SEDUCED BY POWER

THE QUEEN'S CONSORTS: BOOK 3

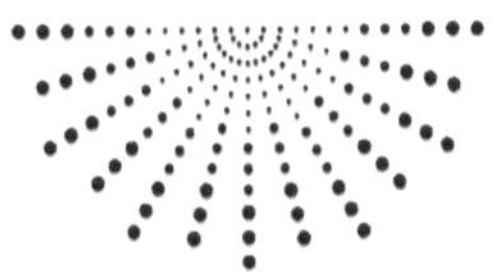

ELENA LAWSON

GET MORE

Join the author's New Releases mailing list and be the first to know when they release a new book. You'll also receive exclusive updates, sneak peaks and freebies.
Visit *www.leamckee.com* to get started.

CHAPTER ONE

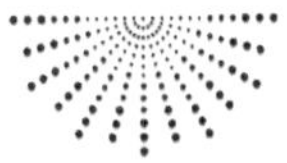

LIANA

Even though it never left the council chamber wall, the edges of the map were yellowed. The canvas-like paper near petrified. I traced the thin line of ink separating the Wastes from the Night Court. That's all it was. A line. And somewhere on the other side, the Mad King was readying his forces to take back the throne.

He wasn't in the ruined palace at Mt. Noctis anymore. We'd checked. And though I'd protested, Kade and Finn had been combing through every inch of the Wastes searching for Ricon's army.

But there was nothing.

Absolutely no trace of this supposed great force Valin had alluded to. And though we still had doubts it even existed, it was time for my court to know the truth. Even without an army, so long as he lived, the Mad Kind would always be a threat.

Tiernan came to stand next to me, considering the top of the map where the Wastes sprawled to the north. Finn looked over his shoulder from the window, but he made no move to join us.

He'd been staring out into the cool autumn evening in brooding silence since we'd gotten to the council chamber. The Draconian looked like a damned gargoyle standing there like that—with his great black wings, corded crossed arms, and dangerous, pensive stare. He seemed to be the most unsettled by it all though I thought it was mostly because he couldn't figure out how to solve the problem. Finn always had the answer, but this time, he didn't.

"It seems so close when you look at it on a map, doesn't it?" Tiernan said, his voice low and brows furrowed.

"The Wastes?"

He shook his head, and the gold in his hair lit like fire in the dying light. "No, the Day Court. But yes—that too."

I wondered if Tiernan missed his home. The vast majority of places on the old map were foreign to me. I knew their names but hadn't the faintest idea what they looked like. I knew the Day Court to be a bright sort of place. The days seemed longer there, the forests were evergreen. It was a place where the earth had never known the cold touch of snow. I knew those things because I'd been told them, but I'd be lying if I said I didn't yearn to see them for myself.

"Do you ever wish to go back?" I asked him, trying to read his drawn expression.

Tiernan inhaled deeply, smirking, "Well," he began, biting his lower lip, "I'll admit I miss the food…. and the wine was a far sight better than what the Night Court has to offer—"

"Tiernan!" I shoved him.

His eyes widened in mock injustice and he rubbed at his wounded shoulder, "You needn't ask," he said more seriously, "I have everything I need right here."

The door to the chamber swung open and Edris strode into the room. "Ah, Your Majesty. Early, I see."

I nodded to the former King Consort, "You may call me by my name when we're without mixed company," I offered him. It was the first I'd seen of the male since we first returned over a week ago. He had seen I was alive and unmarred, heaved a relieved sigh and thanked Alaric—and then he'd left.

I owed him a debt. The only reason I still wore my crown—the only reason no one at court even knew I'd been missing or died was because of him. I wouldn't go so far as to start calling him Father, but, "Thank you," I said to him and watched his eyes widen.

He bowed his head, understanding my meaning, "I owe you that and more, Liana."

Yes, you do, I thought to myself, pulling a chair from the long oval table.

Finn abandoned his brooding at the window, making room for Arrow to land on the ledge. The falcon crooned softly, tucking in his wings to protect his body from the chill. I shook my head at the creature, sighing. It seemed I owed Tiernan's pet my life as well. If it weren't for Arrow showing my males the way to the ruined palace, they may not have found me in time.

The other council members filed into the chamber, their unfinished conversations pouring in with them—echoing off the stone walls. Finn took the chair next to me, and Tiernan stood at my back with his hands clasped at his front. I saw Edris' brows furrow when he realized I had no intention of asking my males to leave.

I really didn't understand why they thought I would follow all their rules. Last I checked, I was their queen. It made little sense that I should have to follow their rules. Besides, Finn was likely smarter than all the fools in the room put together. And Tiernan was more level-headed than most and had the heart of a true warrior.

One by one, the council members took notice of the Draconian and the day-court-emissary-turned-queens-guardian.

The court's baron of finance, a sour-faced male with milky eyes was the first to protest, "Your royal guard has no business attending council meetings."

"Here, here!" said a bearded noble with a golden ring on each of his fingers.

I rolled my eyes.

Silas pulled out a chair and sat. I hadn't seen him since the memorial for the Draconian's who fell at Mt. Ignis, and he looked more tired and pale than I'd ever seen him. I swallowed.

The leader of the Horde armies still hadn't found his sister, and now I had to tell him he never would—unless he was lucky enough to stumble upon her corpse. "Leave them be," he said, "I have other matters to attend to. Let's get this over with."

The others grumbled their discontent but said no more, all except Edris waiting with bitter expressions.

I thought about how to begin. My throat suddenly dry and my shoulders tense. Tiernan placed a warm hand on my shoulder, lending me his strength. Finn gave me a small nod from where he sat, his face grim.

I supposed there was no sense in dancing around the facts.

I cleared my throat and did my best to meet each of their impatient stares.

"The Mad King lives."

I TOLD them what I knew. Tiernan and Finn did their best to help me explain it all. We told them about the missing Fae, and how the Mad King was the one who'd taken them. And how they were now almost certainly dead. We told them about the Blessed Blade, and his plans to take back the Night Court's throne.

We didn't tell them about what happened a week prior. Nor did I feel the need to explain to them about my Graces just yet. They had enough to digest as it was.

Their reactions ranged from blatant disbelief to stupefied awe, to open worry. Edris sat quietly, taking in the information we presented them. Silas' hands were white-knuckled fists atop the table. His jaw tense—his eyes ringed in red.

"You're certain," Silas growled, more a statement than a question.

I nodded, "I'm so sorry."

Silas stood in such a rush his chair flipped over behind him. He took a deep, shaking breath, visibly attempting to calm himself. I applauded the effort. I didn't have a sister, or any siblings save for the one who'd died before I was born, so I didn't know how he felt. But I imagined it was agony trying to maintain composure, "Do we know where his forces are gathering? Or how many lives—how many Graces he's been able to steal?"

I couldn't bring myself to answer him. We knew so little it was pathetic, and the simple word stuck in my throat, not allowing me to utter it. "Um, well—"

"No." It was Finn who answered him, "My brother, and I have combed the entire expanse of the Wastes and found nothing. There were remnants of an abandoned camp near the western shores, but it housed no more than fifty Fae."

"A bluff?" The bearded noble at the other end of the table barked, "Isn't it obvious? You say Valin was the one who told you these things? The bastard was just trying to frighten you."

Silas scowled, "I never liked him."

I shoved my hair away from my sweat-slicked chest, "It isn't a bluff. Trust me."

Silas paced the small space between his chair and the wall, "We send scouts to locate him and this—this *army* of his then—"

"We *have* sent scouts. They've found nothing."

"Then we send more!" Silas stopped, his fists slamming down against the table so hard the wood trembled where I sat.

I inhaled deeply through my nose, "I agree, Silas. We must find him. Until we do, we have no way of knowing what we're dealing with."

A vein jutted out from the war captain's neck, "And when we find him, we'll crush him and his army before they get anywhere near this court."

I chewed the inside of my lip. That would be the best solution, but why did I feel like that wasn't how it would happen? Something about Ricon, and about the way Valin had said he would take back the throne—as though it was the obvious—no, the *only* outcome made me wonder what the Mad King had up his sleeve.

Finn was deep in heated conversation with Silas, explaining exactly where he and Kade had happened upon the abandoned camp, and also every place they'd searched.

There were forests in the Wastes, Silas had suggested. Forests of great pine trees that never lost their needles, and grand leafy trees that formed a ceiling-like canopy over the earth below. "They could be there," Silas said, but they had already searched the forests, and it would be impossible to hide an entire army from sight there, anyway.

We were grasping at straws. And I *knew*—somewhere out there, the Mad King was readying for war while we bickered and fumbled.

"You must ready the Horde armies, Silas," I said, swallowing against the quaking in my chest.

He halted his conversation with Finn, and both men looked at me with a mixture of horror and confusion in their eyes, "Majesty," Silas began, "We have no idea what we're dealing with, here. And until we do—"

"I want my armies ready, Silas," I said, stronger. With no room for argument, "Call them in."

There had been little reason to have our entire army together in centuries. I knew how it worked—more or less. The Horde had five-thousand fighting men and women, but only a thousand were active and training at a time, cycling out with the other four thousand every forty days. There were crops that needed tending, and families that needed feeding.

After almost a thousand years without war, there was no reason to have five-thousand men almost permanently removed from their families.

But now, there was a reason. "Gather the troops," I said, swallowing, "I want them ready within a fortnight."

Silas snorted, "Your Majesty—"

"The queen has decided," Tiernan said, standing. He had been so silent, I'd almost forgotten he was there. "Send your scouts, and see what you can find, and get our forces mustered."

Our forces. The looks on the faces of my council members at Tiernan's use of the word was hard to miss. In their eyes, he would never be a part of *ours* or *us*. A Day Court Fae couldn't ever be.

I shook my head solemnly, "Do as I've asked. Tell them only what they must know and nothing more," I implored Silas. "If I'm wrong, each and every soldier in my army will be paid handsomely for their wasted time."

The baron of finance choked on the wine in his chalice and looked as though he might faint. But he said nothing, just stared at me in horror. The baron might pray I'm right just so we don't bankrupt the kingdom.

But I pray I'm wrong—that it *was* a bluff. That we can find the Mad King and kill him before he's able to raise an army or cause any more harm to the denizens of my court.

Praying has never gotten me anywhere.

CHAPTER TWO

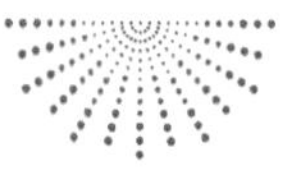

LIANA

The chill evening air pricked like ice against the furnace of my flesh. "That's it," Kade said, "Slowly."

We were training as we'd been doing each day since our return to palace nearly ten days past. And my Graces were becoming easier to control. Fire was still the most difficult, but that was why we trained next to the ocean shore, there was nothing to burn and it was far from anyone who might happen upon us.

The land was wild here. The trees growing in the sand far in the distance gnarled and moss-covered. The shores littered with shells and petrified wood, softened by the eternal tumbling of the ocean's currents.

I pulled at the fire Grace in my core—but gently. As though it were a rabid animal I were coaxing from a dark corner. Afraid it might bite. I lifted my hand and with a small flick of my wrist, a curling orb of flame seeped out from the pores in my skin. Rested, hovering just above my palm.

Kade nodded his approval, "That's it. Now, just a *little* bigger."

This was the part I always struggled with. Once the fire had started, it was quick to grow out of control—just as a forest fire would be. Coaxing miniscule amounts of my Grace forth from my core, I bit down hard on my bottom lip to keep it in check.

The orb swelled as I channeled the heat down through my arm, into my wrist, and out my fingertips. But then the floodgates were open, and I couldn't find the crank to shut them again. My eyes widened at the sudden rush of power, and I aimed my palm away from Kade and Alaric. Blasted the water with a horse-sized ball of leaping, turbulent fire.

The ocean swallowed it. The water simmering and then sputtering, spitting out steam from its surface.

Kade puckered his bottom lip, "Well, it's better than yesterday."

I groaned in frustration, "How long did it take you to control it?" I asked Kade, falling back onto the sand to stare up into the darkening sky.

He clucked his tongue, and Alaric came from where he was watching a safe distance away to sit down next to me, "You really don't want to know," he said.

I rolled my eyes and heaved a great, loud sigh. "Why does everything have to be so damned difficult?"

"Speaking of difficult," Kade said, blocking my view of the red-stained sky with his fat head, "I was thinking," he started, glancing toward Alaric as though the captain may not like what he was about to say, "I think you should train in hand to hand combat. There are times like—like what happened with the bindstone that—well," he stammered, scratching at the back of his head, "What I mean to say is there are times when having that skill is necessary."

And there it was again—that look in his eyes. As though he was hanging from the end of a rope.

Alaric told me to let it be. That he would come out of it and realize the truth on his own—that what happened in the ruined palace was *not* his fault.

Kade wouldn't look at me, and he'd hardly touched me in the days we'd been together since... since I'd died. And if I wasn't mistaken, he'd *thrown* our last game of chess. I had even tried to let him get ahead. Give him a better chance to win, but he'd put himself in a corner—had practically begged me to check his king so the game would be over.

I wanted my Kade back. And he better hurry up because I wasn't sure how much longer I could stand to see him this way.

I turned to Alaric, finding him staring into the wispy clouds on the horizon in pensive, taught, silence. After a time, the tension in his face lessened, and he turned to look at me and Kade, "He's right. It's important that you learn how to defend yourself without the use of your Graces."

It had been months since I'd last trained with the seven sisters on the Isle of Mist. Della had been a weapon embodied in woman-form, but she'd only taught me the basics. What need would a queen have to use that sort of skill? That's what Thana said. Little did I know she was only trying to keep me from growing stronger, so she could do the Mad King's bidding without me putting up too much of a fight.

"It's a good idea," I told Kade, "Will you teach me?"

He snorted, "No, I was thinking Alaric, or maybe Tiernan. Finn and I are good, but we have relied too heavily on our Graces and our ability to fly." He looked a little embarrassed at the admission, "Alaric has been training with the sword since he was a boy, and I've never seen anyone fight like Tiernan—the male moves like water with a sharp edge."

"And your Graces *will* bend to your will, Liana," Alaric said, changing the subject back to the task at hand.

I could tell the very idea of me in close combat with anyone unsettled him to no end. "Finn has been doing more research and after we've all completed the Immortal Bond with you, you should be able to see and *feel* the control we have over our Graces. Mimic it, so to speak. It will be easier."

I picked up a handful of cool sand from my side and watched it slip through my fingers, carried away by the wind. "Why do we have to wait? We should do it now—bond, I mean."

"The bond is strongest when performed under the light of a full moon," Kade reminded me for the hundredth time. I had to question whether he still wanted to bond with me at all by the way he'd said it, "You're bonding with not one, but *four* males—"

"It's never been done before—at least, not to our knowledge. We'll take every advantage we can get to make sure it works," Alaric added.

The half-moon taunted me from its perch high above. It would be days—no *weeks* before it was full. A fortnight—give or take.

Fourteen days

I could wait fourteen more days, right?

Kade stretched out his arms. Rolled his shoulders back and loosened the muscles in his neck. The sun had almost sunk below the line of the horizon, and its burnt orange glow turned his skin a shining bronze. His golden eyes looked brighter against it, and his short brown hair darker.

Alaric stared off with his steel-blue eyes into the churning waves. His strong jaw set, and his brows pulled together in concentrated thought. How I longed to wipe the worry from his features. To see the ecstasy in them like I had that night in my bathing chamber, and later, in my bed.

Fourteen days. I gulped, trying to quell the ache spreading low in my belly and the heat pooling between my thighs.

Just when I was about to say to hell with it and ask them to take me home and ravish me until dawn, the sound of Finn's approach broke the spell—forcing a helping of sense and propriety down my throat.

He swooped down onto the tiny shoreline next to us, cocking his head, "I thought you were training, not napping," he chastised with a smirk.

"Ugh," I groaned, "Just get us home, will you?"

His eyes widened, and he chuckled, "So, you had a productive day, then?"

I rose from the sand, beyond ready to return to the palace, and have myself a very large amount of wine.

Alaric brushed the light sand off his trousers, his black hair falling over his already darkened eyes, "Has Silas sent word yet?" he asked Finn, "Have his scouts uncovered anything?"

The captain of the Horde armies had sent three teams of scouts, two over land and one made up of six Draconians, who searched from the sky. It had only been two days, but combined with the two scout parties Alaric sent out, they should've found *something* by now.

Finn shook his head, "I just came from the Horde camp. And no, there've found nothing."

"It doesn't make any sense," I said, "Why would Valin lie about an attack? They already had me—had planned to kill me—why lie about something like that?"

Alaric pursed his lips, and cleared his throat, "I don't think Valin lied. I believe the Mad King would attempt to reclaim his throne. And even with his abilities, he would have to take it by force—he'd have to have a very large army to even dream of taking on the Horde."

I shivered.

"That's the most confusing part," Finn said, pulling me into his arms and rubbing soothing circles into my back.

I tilted my head up to look at him, "What is?"

"Like Alaric said, Ricon would have to have a sizeable force to have a chance at succeeding, but what I don't understand is *where* he would get a force that large. There are some Fae who live in the Wastes. There are small villages, but that's all."

Alaric said, "They number only in the hundreds. Not thousands."

"Exactly," Finn nodded, and I understood why he was so confused. Even if the Mad King were able to gather every Fae in all the Wastes, he would only have an army of perhaps a thousand, and they would not be warriors—he'd have an army of simple folk. Farmers. Peasants, and the scourge that lived within caves in the mountains.

"We'll figure it out," Kade said, tossing a large rock up and down in hand, his gaze fixed on the spot where the sun had just slipped below the water, "He'll have to show his ugly face sometime right?" He shrugged and threw the stone far out to sea.

Finns arms tensed around me.

Alaric walked over to Kade, "We should get back."

"Wait," Finn said, his gaze roving over the sea, "That's it."

I stepped back from him, "What is?"

"We can't find Ricon's army because it isn't here," he said animatedly, his eyes alight, "Can't you see," he said, gesturing to the view before us. "We've combed over every inch of the Wastes and found nothing. The abandoned camp was on the western shore. And there aren't enough Fae he'd be able to rally to fight for his cause on Meloran."

He wouldn't have...

No, it wasn't possible. Was it?

Kade's jaw dropped, and Alaric's eyes hardened.

"He's gathering his forces, alright," Finn continued, "And he's bringing them here by sea."

"That's why we couldn't find them," Kade said, a faraway look in his eyes, "We can't fly that far out to sea without rest."

Alaric ran a fisted hand through his hair, "So how do we find out? Do we send ships to scout on the seas?"

Finn shook his head, "It would take our entire fleet to find them if that's where they are. The Varinian Sea is just too vast."

"We can do it," Kade said, his hands balling to fists at his sides, "We can fly further. Our ancestors flew all the way to Emeris—to Mt. Idris. We can at least fly half as far."

Alaric frowned at Kade, "No, Kade. You can't shift like they could. You'll drown if you try."

"I have an idea," I said, rolling the thought around in my mind, trying to work it into a proper shape.

Finn stepped away from me, "Alaric is right," he said to Kade, "It would be sui—"

"I *said* I have an idea," I said again, louder.

Alaric turned to me, "What was that?"

I rolled my eyes at him, the heat at my core reawakening to a light simmer, "The Wraiths," I said simply.

"The Wraiths warned me about Ricon, and they saved your life,"

I said, looking pointedly at Finn, "If I ask them, I think they'll help us. There are hundreds of them in the Varinian sea and they communicate through their minds. They can have the entirety of the sea searched in days instead of weeks."

Alaric and Kade wore twin frowns, but Finn nodded his approval, "You're a genius," he said, turning to scoop me up off the earth and into a suffocating embrace.

He plopped me back down and I heaved air back into my lungs. When my breath returned, I shoved him, "Not so hard!"

Finn bit his bottom lip, and the motion made me instantly lose all my ire. I shook my head at him. My sweet, smart Finn. What would I do without him? "So, it's agreed then?" I asked him, "We should go to the Wraiths for help."

Alaric kicked at the sand, thrusting his fisted hands into the pockets of his trousers, "I don't like it, but even I can't deny it's a good plan."

Kade shivered, "Those things are so—"

"So?" I prodded him.

"Gross."

"Gross?"

He swallowed, "They're all—slimy and tentacley."

"Tentacley?"

He nodded, "And they're *blue*."

I choked on a laugh, wanting to kiss the ridiculous scowl from his face. But in his current state of everything-is-all-my-fault he might not return the sentiment, "Come on, lets go home. We have an offering to make ready."

CHAPTER THREE

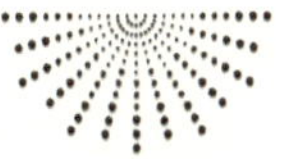

LIANA

It was widely known that the Wraiths of the Varinian Sea were enamored by all things fine. Pearls, jewels, gold. Finn had given them an offering of a black pearl necklace after they'd saved his life. It was said they had a trove of such treasures somewhere deep in the ocean. In a chasm that had no bottom.

"What about this?" Finn suggested, holding up a chain of pure gold. It was a fine piece of jewelry, but it wasn't enough. It was no small undertaking we were asking of them. It would take all of them working together to find the Mad King's fleet—if he did in fact have one—within such a short amount of time. Which was why we were raiding the palace treasury instead of my own dressing table. We needed something *big*.

Alaric and Kade were less inclined to trust the Wraiths and were getting precautionary weapons ready. Spears and bows, apparently. In case the wild creatures turned on us. There was no talking them out of it. Stubborn males.

"This?" Finn asked again, digging into the open maw of an aged wooden chest. He pulled out a length of fat pearls.

They were beautiful, but, "No, still not enough."

"What do you propose then," he said, cocking his head at me. In the torchlight I noticed the slight stubble on his jaw. Kade occasionally let his grow to stubble, but never Finn. It was odd seeing the shadow on his cheeks and under his chin. It made his features more rugged—less sharp. It suited him.

I looked around the grand room. There were shelves upon shelves of treasures. Chests of gold pieces and jewels. Tables laden with every manner of fine jewelry. But it was a bright red glow across the chamber that caught my eye.

It stood proud atop a stand of polished silver. A stone the size of my fist, red as blood and cut so it reflected light. "What about that?" I asked Finn, pointing to the giant gemstone.

Finn looked at me as though I'd grown another head, "That ruby is worth more than my entire village—no, actually it's probably worth more than *all* the villages in the north combined."

"It's perfect."

"You're insane."

I smirked at him, and walked over to the table, admiring the way the gen fractured the light into a gauzy red glow. "It's heavy," I said in surprise as I lifted it from the silver stand. It was so large, I couldn't even wrap my fingers around it.

"Don't tell the baron of finance about this?"

Finn's eyes widened, and he barked a nervous laugh, "No, don't think I will. He'd have my head on a platter if he knew I let you take that."

I stepped in close to him, slipping the ruby into the pocket of his jacket, "Our secret, then."

"You're wicked," he said, and drew my body against his. His eyes glazed with lust.

My pulse sped, forcing a blush up my neck. His hands brushed the curves of my back—my waist, and his breathing became labored. I brushed my lips against the soft skin of his collarbone, and his body shook. I wondered how long it'd been since he'd lain with a woman.

"I'm sorry," I whispered against his skin, and he shivered even more.

He took my chin into his hand and narrowed his gaze at me, "No you're not."

I shook my head, smiling, "No—you're right. I'm not." And then I kissed him, taking in his parchment and clove scent and the intoxicating feel of his cool fingers as they ran through my hair, and gently stroked the sensitive spot under my jaw.

I had meant the kiss to be playful, to take some worry from his shoulders—but it wasn't playful. It was scorching hot. And freezing cold. So sweet and tender, but also insistent and frantic. When he finally pulled away from me his eyes were vibrant gold, shining with untamed desire, and something like fear.

"You will be the death of me," he breathed, and brushed an unruly strand of hair away from my cheek.

I kissed him again, this time on the cheek, "I certainly hope not."

Coming back to himself, he noticed the golden chain had fallen to the floor and stooped to pick it up. He moved to put it into a chest, but I stopped him, pulling the chain from his fingertips. It was well-crafted, strong, a necklace fit for a king. I struggled with the clasp but was finally able to unfasten it.

"Turn around," I said to Finn, who had his hands held up as though I was mad.

"What are you doing?" he asked, trying to back away. But I grabbed hold of his outstretched hands and pulled him close, fastening the chain around his neck in one quick movement.

"There," I said, admiring my handiwork. The chain looked so much smaller around his neck than it had in my small hands. It brought out the gold in his eyes, and the umber tones of his skin.

Finn snickered at me but rubbed the chain with his fingertips as though it were the most precious thing in the world. And was he *blushing*?

"I really shouldn't—"

I hushed him, "Yes, you *should*. It's a gift, Finn. You look as though no one has ever given you one."

"They haven't," he said, looking everywhere but at me, "Not since I was a child."

My heart ached at the darkened expression on his face, "Come on," I said, taking him by the hand, "Let's go find the others, they'll be waiting for us."

Finn nodded, "Right," he said, squeezing my hand, "We should go, but Liana…" he trailed off.

"Yes?"

"Thank you," he said.

I made a noncommittal sound, trying to brush off his thanks, but he wasn't having it.

"I mean it," he said more forcefully, "I'll never take it off."

"Took you long enough," Kade said, holding a spear almost twice his height in his left hand.

Alaric spun from where he was standing on the cliff-side, sighing in relief, a quiver of arrows and a bow slung across his back. "We were starting to worry."

Tiernan narrowed his gaze at Finn, his focus zeroing in on Finn's neck, "Did a little shopping, I see."

"If you want a gift, too, all you have to do is ask," I teased.

"Ok, I'm asking. I want one, too."

"Done." I winked at him, stepping up to the cliffs edge to peer over the side. Tiernan pulled me back.

"Maybe don't lean over the edge of a hundred yard cliff, alright?"

Alaric sighed, "If you're finished," he said, giving Tiernan and I a pointed look, "Could we please get this over with?"

Right. None of us wanted to be there. To have to ask the Wraiths for help to find the armed forces of a Mad King who was bent on my destruction.

Godsforbid I get even a moments peace on this damned continent.

"Let's go," I said, and stepped into Finn's arms with Tiernan. Kade sprinted, grabbing hold of Alaric under his arms before he dove from the cliff.

"Ready?" Finn asked, and I held tighter to Tiernan, and tighter around Finn's waist. Nodded.

He let his body fall from the ledge, and my stomach jumped into my throat. He waited three blissful seconds before he fanned out his wings and soared over the surface of the water, chasing after his brother.

The Wraiths weren't known to frequent many places except the fathomless deeps where they stored their treasures—though no one knew exactly where that was—but they were seen now and again near a tiny unnamed isle just a few miles from the coast. That was where we headed. Flying low under the cover of night so we didn't draw attention to ourselves.

Alaric suggested I wait at the palace—that they could handle asking the Wraiths themselves. Thank the gods I had Finn there to back me up. The seas were vast, and yet the Wraiths had found me not once, but twice. If I was right, they could somehow *sense* my presence when I was near the water. Finn agreed.

Besides, they were much more likely to aid a request if it came directly from a queen. They were an ungoverned race—without a true leader of their own. They traveled in groups, mostly. *Packs.* There was an alpha and a beta in each, but no one pack was superior to another. They all lived together in the chasm in the deeps.

So, though Alaric—and Kade, hated the idea. *I* was the one who'd have to do the asking.

The tiny isle came into view moments later. Nothing more than a cluster of rock, moss, and dirt, with a few shrubs and trees speckled near the center.

I swallowed, a miasmal feeling creeping over my skin at the chill in the air and the sight of the hard gray stone bathed in moonlight.

I hoped this was the right thing to do. But most of all, I hoped Finn was wrong—and the Wraiths proved it.

The Draconian set Tiernan and I down atop the uneven earth. Without the wind rushing past us, it was eerily quiet. I hadn't real-ized Arrow had followed us until his screech broke the silence and had me tripping over my own feet. Finn caught me before I fell backwards into the water.

I threw the creature a cutting glance as it landed atop the lowest branch of a naked tree. Squawking like a gull.

"Damn you, Arrow," I cursed at him. He ruffled his feathers, turning himself so I was faced with his tail. Cheeky little bugger.

Tiernan shook his head, "I hardly see him anymore," he mused, "Where have you been?" he asked his pet, as if the falcon could answer him.

"Stalking me—that's where he's been," I said, righting myself, waiting for Kade and Alaric to make their way to us over the stones and moss.

"Good boy," Tiernan said. Arrow cooed, turning back around.

"Ready?" Alaric said, gesturing to the water at our backs when he and Kade approached.

"I am," I said, "Did you see any when we were flying in?" I asked —the question meant for all of them.

"No," said Finn, "They don't come up to the surface often."

Alaric, Kade, and Finn all shook their heads as well.

"Time to put the theory to the test then." I pulled my hair back and tied it with a strip of leather from my wrist.

"You stay here," I said—mostly to Kade and Alaric, "You'll only scare them off."

Alaric laughed roughly, "If you think I'm letting you go in that water *alone*, you're insane."

"You aren't *letting* me do anything," I said, a little more abrasive than I'd intended, "I'm going in the water and you're staying here," I said, trying to soften my voice.

Alaric set his jaw, ready to come back with some scathing retort, but Finn turned and stepped into the water, "I'll go with her," he offered, "If that's alright with you," he added, posing the question to me.

They had helped save Finn once, and he had no weapons on him aside from his sword. I nodded, "Alright, but take that off. I don't want them to fear us."

He did as I asked and unbuckled his entire belt. Tossed it onto the ground, the sword clanging against the stones.

"I don't like this," Alaric grumbled, stepping in to stop me.

His eyes gleamed in the moonlight like polished silver. "I'll be alright," I told him, "Finn will be right beside me, and I know you're an incredible shot with that bow."

"Are you trying to ply me with compliments?"

"Is it working?"

He smirked, running his fingers through my hair, "So damned stubborn," he said under his breath, "Just be careful."

I turned to where Finn waited, one boot in the water and the other still on shore. I took his outstretched hand, kicking off my own shoes before I stepped into the sea.

The water was a shock to my skin. Autumn had turned it from bearable to near-freezing. I radiated a little heat from my core, letting it spread through my skin. As long as I didn't open the gates and let it out, it would remain only as a warm ember and nothing more.

I cringed as my toes squished into the slimy, pebbled seabed, stepping on tip-toe to avoid as much of it as I was able.

"Watch your step—it drops off in another few yards."

He was right. The water was just above waist level, and ahead I saw where the bottom we walked on vanished into darkness. Another two steps and we'd be in over our heads.

"Now what?" Finn asked.

I shrugged, "I suppose we wait."

CHAPTER FOUR

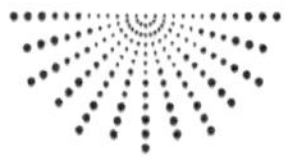

FINN

We didn't have to wait long. But I was glad I was the one who offered to go in with her. Liana had her Grace of fire to keep her warm, but if she knew how to properly harness her Grace of ice, she would find the cold wouldn't bother her at all. She had more ice and cold within her than there could ever be in the sea. She would be with me for her next training session, and I would teach her how.

Within ten minutes we could see them coming in the distance. Their translucent skin glowed blueish silver in the moonlight, like the squids we used to jig off the docks as young children. Writhing, shimmering things.

Kade was right, they were a little... off-putting, but their beauty was greater than their strangeness.

Liana stiffened as they drew near. It was a small group of maybe six or seven. One lead the others in a triangle-like formation until they were mere yards away from where we stood.

I heard Alaric notch an arrow, and Liana spun to glare at him, "Idiot," she hissed at him, "Put that away."

I bit back a laugh.

The Wraiths were a strange—but peaceful creature. Truly, we

had nothing to fear from them. Though many folk blamed them for any and all deaths that happened at sea. I supposed it was easier to have something to blame than never knowing why a loved one sailed off and never returned.

Liana swallowed, watching the Wraiths as they raised themselves up closer to the surface, she glanced at me and I saw the anxiety in the set of her jaw and the widening of her eyes. "It's alright, we've only come to ask a favor. If they refuse, we'll find another way."

She nodded, catching her bottom lip between her teeth.

The leading Wraith raised its head from the water. Slitted black eyes looked from Liana to me and back again. The creature's hair was wild undulating silver and its small, sharp-angled face glowed silvery blue.

"I have come to ask something of you," Liana began, her hands clasped tightly at her front and her shoulders set.

….what will the Queen of Night ask of us… The Wraith asked.

I jolted at the intrusion in my mind. The words scraped along the inside of my skull. I gritted my teeth against the feeling.

Liana stumbled, tripping over her words, "We must—we are seeking to know if…"

"It's possible there is a fleet of ships, either docked on the eastern shores of Emeris, or bound for Meloran. Those ships would be carrying men and Fae and their aim is to end Morgana's line and take the throne of night."

Liana mouthed *thank you* to me once I'd finished, some tension in her shoulders abated.

…the Mad King…

"Yes," Liana said. "We must find him. We must know how many fighting soldiers he has in his army."

…What you ask of us…

"I ask that you find them."

The Wriaths eyes narrowed to tiny slits, and it made a hissing sound through its thin lips….*kill them?…*

The other Wraiths behind the first one raised their heads from the water too, hissing and swaying back and forth.

"Liana," Alaric warned.

Tiernan's falcon screeched.

"It's fine," she called back to Alaric, but her resolve was weakening.

I drew on my Grace, coaxing it out from the center of my being in case I should have need of it. I took her hand, trying to lend her some of my strength.

"No," she said to the creatures as she turned back to face them, "I would not ask that of you."

...we help you. We help the queen...

"You will search the seas?" I asked the Wraith, ensuring the primitive creature understood our request, "And you will tell us what you find?"

No answer.

"Oh, here," Liana said, pulling the ruby from her vest. "A gift."

Liana let go of my hand, moving to the edge of the drop-off. The Wraith came to meet her there. I clenched my hands into fists to keep from following her. I didn't want to scare the creature and ruin her plans.

She's fine. She'll be fine.

Liana held out the gem for the creature, and it reached out with a thin arm and snatched it from her hand with small webbed fingers. Its black eyes widened at the sight. Then it moved away, it's tentacles propelling it backwards.

I sighed in relief.

...three days... The Wraith's scratching voice said in my mind. *...we return to this place...*

"Meet you here, in only three days? Is that enough time?" I asked.

...time?... We are many, winged male...we find the ships...

The Wraith blinked its double eyelids, and I heard Kade make a disgusted sound behind us.

I wondered how he was holding up. He didn't like to admit, but he'd had a run-in with a Wraith once as a younger male. I don't know how he thought fire would win out over water when he dove in off the docks to catch one. He'd come back up sputtering and rubbing at his skin as though it were covered in acid instead of a bit of algae and a couple angry red tentacle marks.

"Thank you. I will not forget this," Liana said to the Wraiths, bowing to them to show her gratitude. I did the same.

...three days... The lead Wraith reminded us and then sank back under the water and the seven of them disappeared like streaks of moonlight into the deeps.

CHAPTER FIVE

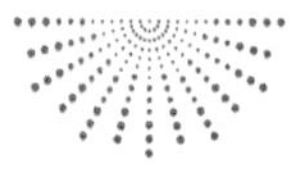

LIANA

He'd tied back his golden hair. Wearing nothing more than a light tunic and his trousers. No shoes. No armor. And yet Tiernan looked more like a warrior than any male I'd ever seen as he circled me in the ring. His muscles taught, and eyes focused on me like a predator. He waited for me to initiate the attack.

I watched his movements, how one step crossed over the other as we circled each other. How his arms were raised, ready to block an attack. He didn't have a weak point. We'd been at this for over an hour and he hadn't even broken a sweat.

My hair stuck to my neck and back where the long ponytail brushed against my skin and the small hairs at my neckline broke free from the leather band. Sweat beaded on my chest and dripped between my breasts. I had three new bruises, though they were healing quickly even without the use of my healing Grace.

It was because of my healing Grace that I told him not to go easy on me. I could heal any injury he gave me so long as he didn't break any bones.

I'd likely need Healer Loris' help to heal that and the old crone has been recluse and extra bitter since we told her Aisling wouldn't be returning. My eyes pricked at the mere thought of her. I tried to shake off the feeling, but it lingered in bones. A heavy, hollowness.

Focus, I demanded of myself.

I lunged, quick as I could, spinning at the last second to use the force of gravity to make the kick more forceful. He caught my leg and threw me back. I stumbled but stayed upright.

"Not fast enough," he said, his green eyes shining. Challenging me. "And you must hit harder. Remember to use your full body weight—that's the only way you'll be able to do any damage. And don't aim *for* me—"

"Aim *through* you," I finished for him, "I know."

"Then do it," he taunted, and I lunged forward again, feinting left before going right, raising an elbow to his throat. Using the force of my entire right side to make the blow stronger. He ducked at the last second and I sailed through the air until he kicked my legs from under me and I fell to the sandy ground.

I grunted past the pain, trying to regain my breath. Gritting my teeth. Fire raged to life in my core as my frustration took hold.

Tiernan tsked, "No Graces," he reminded me, taking a cursory look around the outskirts of the sparring ring. We hadn't used it since before we even knew about my Graces. We had to practice those in private now, but for hand to hand combat training, we could have an audience. So, an audience we had.

I tried to ignore them like Tiernan said, and it had been working, but when I fell yet again, I heard their gasps and whispers. Some worried I would be hurt. Others whispered how weak I was. But the vast majority seemed put off by the fact I was sparring at all—and in trousers no less. As if I should spar in a gown. Because *that* wouldn't be a hindrance at all… did they think I couldn't hear them?

"Just order them away," Tiernan said, stepping in to help me stand.

His mistake. I grabbed hold of his forearm and threw a kick into his abdomen, using the strength in my legs to lift his feet from the sand. Tossing him over my body to land with a *hmphh* on his head.

Dazed, he stood, trying to find his balance.

The crowd cheered.

I smiled.

But he swayed, and I saw the dizziness in his eyes. Had he fallen that hard?

"Tiernan?" I asked, "Are you alright?"

He barrelled into me as though he were a rogue wave. His shoulder connecting with my breastbone, expelling all the breath from my lungs. I fell back, gasping, and he landed atop me. Stradling me. Pinning my arms painfully hard against my sides.

I looked up to find a cheeky grin and lustful eyes staring into mine. My body ached everywhere, and I was still struggling for breath, but he didn't yield.

"Give up?"

I swallowed something that tasted like blood in my mouth. My lip throbbed. I must've bitten it. I shook my head at him. "You bastard," I said between panting breaths.

"I'll take that as a yes," he said, and stood, offering me a hand.

I took it, and he pulled me from the ground.

"You did well," he said, "You're more skilled than I thought you would be."

"Show's over!" I hollered at the gathering of nobles and servants watching us. They scattered like mice.

Tiernan's eyes lingered on the glistening sweat coating the mounds of my breasts. He licked his lips.

"I'm sorry if I hurt you," he said, and I looked down to see an ugly bruise spreading over my breastbone below my tunic.

Focusing on the healing Grace and drawing on its warm, soothing power, I healed the bruise in the matter of a minute, and all the other marks Tiernan had riddled my body with.

"There," I said, opening my eyes, "It's as though it never happened."

He smiled, but it didn't reach his eyes. He would do as I asked him because he knew going soft on me would teach me nothing, but I saw how it affected him.

Tiernan peeked down the front of my tunic, seemed pleased

with what he found there, "Alright," he said. "But I'd still like to make it up to you."

I cocked my head at him, catching his true meaning.

"How do you intend to do that?"

"It would be easier if I showed you…" he trailed off, "Can I escort you back to your chambers?"

THE INSTANT the door to my bedchamber shut behind us, Tiernan locked his lips onto mine, shoving me roughly against the wooden grain of the door. He had my tunic untied and over my head within seconds. His own threadbare shirt fell to the floor, too.

His tongue parted my lips, slipping into my mouth. Hot and insistent.

He pulled away, his gaze boring into my soul. "I can't wait for the ceremony," he said, his voice husky and deep. "I was going to try, but I can't."

I yanked him back, pressing my bare breasts against his chest. His hair came loose from the tie, and I reached up and yanked it free. Grabbed a fistful of it.

"Then don't," I said, and he growled, descending upon me like an animal.

My legs were around his waist, and he lifted me onto him. I could feel his hardened length pressing against me, begging to be freed from the confines of his trousers. He dropped me onto the bed and stood back to admire me as I lay there, shirtless, and panting.

"You are incredible," he said, his eyes wild and hungry. Slowly, like a cat readying to pounce, he knelt before me, tugging my legs to the edge of the bed. He undid the fastenings of my trousers and peeled them from my sweat-dampened skin. The thin silk panties I wore beneath were already soaked with hot, silky moisture.

He pinched either side at my waist and pulled them off— maddeningly slow.

I moaned, arching my back. Trying to get closer to him. To urge him to move faster.

"Tiernan," I whispered, a plea.

I lifted my head to find him with his lips parted, his mouth mere inches from my sex. His warm breath brushing against it. He kissed the inside of my thigh and I whimpered. He kissed the other side and my body shook.

"I want to taste you," he said, and his mouth closed over my clit. My hips bucked as his tongue flicked against the sensitive spot. Over and over and *over.* The quickening began, and I had to fight to keep from crushing his head between my thighs. My legs twining around his head.

"Not yet," he said, and I shoved his head back down.

"Don't you dare stop," I said between panting breaths.

My muscles tightened and contracted as I moved my hips to the rhythm of his tongue.

Almost…

As though he knew I were about to lose myself he moved expertly fast. Flipping me over, and sheathing himself inside me in one quick, hard thrust.

CHAPTER SIX

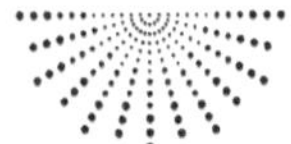

TIERNAN

I drove my cock into her, gripping her by her hips. She trembled beneath me and I watched her slight hands curl into the soft linens like talons. Her hair splayed like liquid silver over the unmarked flesh of her back. She ground her hips against me as I thrusted. Her sharp moans driving me to the brink.

Her silky wetness—and that *heat* inside her… I hoped she could keep her Grace of fire at bay because there wasn't anything in the world that would make me stop. I'd let myself burn before I stopped.

Liana. My Liana.

I'd had my fair share of females, but none had this effect on me. This dizzying, chaotic sensation. I'd tied them up. Made them beg for *their* release. And now I was near ready to beg for my own.

Not her. Not my *queen*. I'd never tie her down, or make her beg… Not unless she wanted me to. No, I would give her every possible ounce of pleasure I could.

I dug my fingers into the flesh at her waist, trying to stall my own satisfaction. Not yet. Not until she was shaking. Not until I made her forget her own name. I reached around her, slipping my fingers along her skin from navel to clit. She gasped at the dual sensation. I pressed two fingers to her, circling the tender flesh of her mound, finding just the right spot that would undo her.

Her breaths came quicker, harder, and I thrusted harder and deeper, never ceasing the quick circular motions of my fingers. She tightened around my cock. The sound of her release was a crescendo. She shuddered, her entire body quivering as she came.

But I didn't stop, I only slowed, letting her ride the wave of her ecstasy.

Gods, the small sounds she made tormented me. My cock throbbed inside her and I didn't think I could wait much longer.

She pushed herself back, forcing me deeper, urging me for more.

I lifted her leg from the bed and over me until we faced one another. Her eyes were glazed with passion. She yanked me to her and my lips found hers as I moved inside her with alternatingly slow and then *quick* jabs.

She was close, I could feel it. Her nails bit down into the tight skin of my back and the pain was exquisite.

"Come with me," I whispered in her ear and her body tightened as I came inside her—finding our release together in a mass of tangled limps and shuddering, broken breaths.

I AWOKE to find the sun already on its path down the sky to slumber. Alaric would kill me if he knew I'd fallen asleep while on watch, thank the gods he hadn't already arrived to relieve me. I reached out for Liana, wanting her closer, but my hands came up empty.

I bolted upright, my blood chilling. Where had she gone? Throwing the covers and pillows from the bed, I found it empty. The door to her chamber remained closed. I'd have heard it open, wouldn't I? Not in her bathing chamber, either.

Where did she... I saw it. The seam in the wall where the secret passageway loomed behind the hewn stone walls. Alaric wanted to have it sealed up, but Finn had argued having it sealed would only draw more attention to its existence, since it was clear no one had used any of the passageways in hundreds of years.

I shook my head, tugging on my trousers, boots, and vest. Raced into the passageway. The darkness swallowed me whole after only a few feet and I fumbled through the blindness until my hands closed over a torch set in a sconce on the wall. I pulled it out and used a stone from the ground to strike a spark and light it.

"Liana," I called, but only the skitter of rats and a *drip drip, drip drip,* answered me. Cursing, I searched the ground and found her footprints leading off into the gloom. She was barefoot, and I was lucky there was a fine layer of stone dust on the floor of the tunnel to show which way she went. My right hand twitched into a fist and my breathing turned ragged.

Why would she leave without waking me? And why—or *how* had I even allowed myself to fall asleep in the first place? I never slept with females—bedded them, yes, but never slept with them afterwards. There was foul play at work, I was sure of it.

Her footprints were staggered, as though she were drunk, and I followed them quickly and silently. I said a silent thanks to whichever gods would listen that there was only one set of footprints. *She's alone,* I thought, at least she hadn't been taken. For whatever reason, she'd gone of her own accord.

See? It's alright. She's alright. I'm alright. Everything *is fine.*

She had turned right, and then right again and then left. It had to have been nearing a half hour since leaving her chamber by the time I came upon a set of stone stairs leading downward. The air in the passageway was cool, but the air coming from below was colder still, and my panting breaths puffed in great clouds of steam around my face.

She went down there. She must've. Her prints left a wobbling trail on each step.

My blood chilled.

Breathing deeply to keep a clear mind, I raced down them two at a time. There was light up ahead, and I threw down my torch, trading it in for my blade, my pulse franticly beating against the bones of my ribcage.

"Liana," I called, running down the last few steps. I faltered when

I got to the bottom, dogged by the grandness of the wide, domed chamber before me. Dragons crouched for the kill, their faces snarled and hissing. And Morgana was there too, standing amidst them, her hands outstretched and face as calm and placid as Lake Serin.

At her feet, within the stone dragon barrier knelt Liana, rocking forward and back, her shoulders trembling.

Swallowing, I sheathed the sword. It was the chamber her and Finn had described. She'd found it again, but why had she come back?

"Liana?" I said, hesitant, approaching her with caution. I double-checked the surrounding chamber, ensuring there was no one else within before I ran the last few yards and knelt beside her. "Liana," I said, laying a hand on her shoulder, jerking it back when my skin met hers. Her flesh was like ice and seemed covered in a thin layer of frost. She made no indication of knowing I was there.

Her head remained bowed, and she continued her slow rocking.

Moving in front of her, I took her frozen face into my hands, tilting it up to the light. It took me a moment to realize she was asleep.

"I need you to wake up, love," I begged, trying to stay calm. Her eyes were closed, and twin streams of tears ran down her cheeks, freezing into drops of ice against her skin.

She was dreaming—having a nightmare.

I shook her softly, "You have to wake up," I said, but she didn't stir. "Liana, wake up," I said, louder—near shouting. But still she did not wake.

Forgive me, I thought, my stomach twisting, before I slapped her cheek as hard as I dared.

She came back to herself with wide blinking eyes and hands raised, searching for something solid to hold onto. "Don't!" she screamed.

CHAPTER SEVEN

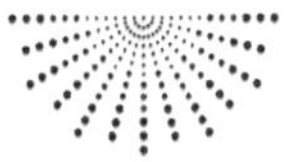

LIANA

*T*iernan's worried jade eyes came into focus as I surfaced from the pull of the dream. I tried to blink away the remnants of it, but fragmented pieces remained, flashing behind my eyelids every time I closed them. Blood, fire, ash, and smoke. The screaming—it was everywhere, interrupted only by the deafening *clash* of steel and the roaring of thunder in the black clouds above.

"Don't what?" Tiernan said, and my cheek stung as my consciousness found its way down from the clouds and back into my body.

"Ouch," I said, rubbing at the sore spot with numbed fingers. Wondered why I was so cold. Why I seemed to be barefoot.

"Sorry about that—you—well, I think you were sleepwalking."

I swallowed past a lump in my throat and looked up, gasping and scrambling backward when I saw Morgana's regal face looking down on me.

"Hey, it's alright," Tiernan said, moving to comfort me.

I let him pull me to him, let him rub warmth back into my arms. "Shhhh… come on, let's get you back to your chambers."

"How did I get down here?" I heard myself ask though the question was mostly for myself.

Tiernan scooped me up into his arms, shivering against the chill of my body, "I'm not sure, but I think maybe you walked here in your sleep." He pulled me closer to his chest, and I curled my arms around his neck, "I'm sorry, Liana. I—I barely remember closing my eyes. I shouldn't have fallen asleep."

"There's nothing to apologize for," I whispered against him, reveling in the feel of his warmth, "I'm alright."

But I wasn't sure if that was true… was I alright?

I closed my eyes against the warmth seeping into my bones and was assaulted with more fragmented pieces of the dream. A ridge covered in shadow from the dark clouds. The *crack* of thunder in my ears. Blood on my hands. I snapped my eyes open, frost bloomed at my fingertips. My blood roared through my veins, spurred by the chaotic beating of my heart. I worked to calm myself, but I was so weak—so tired. Tiernan shivered again, pulling me in as tight as he could to share his body heat.

The stairway wavered in and out of focus as he carried me, and I flinched when he bent to pick up a torch from the ground. The light too bright for my eyes.

Strange, that I had been sleeping not long before. I couldn't think of a time when I had ever been so tired. I longed for my bed. And the comfort I only felt in the company of all my men. I needed to see them all—that they were safe and unharmed—yes, I would see them safe, and then I would sleep.

I tried to draw on my Grace of fire but found ice at my core instead. The fire unable to penetrate the thick wall of it shrouding my heart.

TIERNAN TOLD the others what happened, though at my request, he left out the part about having found me distraught and cocooned in fear. *No more secrets,* I had promised them all.

Since sleepwalking was a new occurrence, and one they should all be aware of in case I walked myself right off the terrace or walked my way out the palace. But they didn't need to know what I had dreamt.

I hardly knew what I dreamt. Bits and pieces of the nightmare came back to me, but the bulk of it was lost to the dark recesses of my mind, as though the dream itself were a nocturnal creature, running from the light.

I don't know what Alaric would have done to Tiernan if I hadn't asked him not to punish my guardian. He was *seething* when Tiernan told him he'd fallen asleep, and I was glad I was there, still half in and half out of consciousness when Tiernan told his captain. It was clear as crystal to see how Tiernan already punished himself for his moment of carelessness, he didn't need to be punished more. I was glad Alaric saw it too—or *felt* it.

Kade held me loosely in his arms as we waited on the tiny island off the coast of the palace. It had been a day since Tiernan carried me all the way back to my royal bedchamber, careful to seal the passageway in the wall behind him and place my armoire in front of it. There was no way I'd ever been able to move it alone—no more sleepwalking in dark, forgotten passageways for me.

And it had been three days since the Wraith agreed to help us and search the seas for a possible threat against us. Now we waited for the Wraiths to return, under a moon that was on the fuller side of half.

"Where are they?" Alaric asked, "They should have been here by now. They're late."

"Maybe they forgot," offered Tiernan.

Finn huffed, "Small chance of that—they are wise creatures, with memories that can go back hundreds of years. They would not forget the events of three nights past."

Kade said nothing, but he sighed against me. I turned around in his arms, "Hey," I said laying a hand on his cheek, "Are you alright?"

He gave me a wan smile and a small nod, "Of course. I'm fine."

I swallowed back the burning bits my throat. He had that look again, the same one he'd been wearing off and on since we returned to the palace. In his eyes I saw another Kade, a Kade that hung from a noose of his own making. Suffocating and in pain.

I opened up my senses, searching for the sixth sense Alaric had been training me to use. Sometimes I felt their emotions by accident, and sometimes, when I didn't have the Grace activated, I felt nothing from them at all. He was teaching me to invite the emotions of others in, but only when I wanted to feel them.

And how to block them out when I didn't.

I reached through my flesh and *felt* Kade with my Grace. I recoiled at the blow of his raw emotion. He was in anguish. On the verge of collapse. He hadn't been the same since that day in the ruins of the old palace. I understood why, but I wouldn't accept it. Alaric told me to leave him be—that he needed time to process what had happened and realize the truth on his own—that he had nothing to do with my death.

Gods! I was standing here, wasn't I? What was there to mope about?

"You have to stop," I said, forcing him to look at me, "Do you hear me?"

His dark brows pulled together, and his adams apple bobbed. "What—"

"You know exactly what I'm talking about."

"Liana—"

"Be quiet and listen," I said, pulling him back when he tried to pull away, "You did nothing wrong. You were not in control of yourself—"

"I don't think—" Finn warned, stepping in to break us apart.

I gave him a sharp glare that had him backing away instead. "I saw what happened, Kade. I was there. I know what Ricon did to you. Why can't you see it wasn't your faul—"

Kade set his jaw, "Oh and you think you know everything, do you?" He grabbed my forearms and glared into my eyes. His own golden eyes glowed, and I felt the heat of his Grace awakening where his skin touched mine. "You have no idea what it was like!"

"Then tell me."

"I almost killed Alaric, and that was bad enough. I'd have never forgiven myself. He controlled me, *yes*, but *I* gave in to his will. *I* was not strong enough," fury gleamed in his eyes and heat rippled off him in waves. I activated my own Grace of fire to keep from burning where his molten fingers circled my arms. "And then... *I* killed *you*."

"Yes," I said, "*You did*."

His eyes widened, and his grip on my arms loosened enough for me to pull myself from them. "Now you listen to me, Kade. I'm *done* seeing you like this. If it had been me who wielded the sword and I had killed *you*, would you hold it against me?"

"No, of course I w—"

"Exactly. And if I were distraught over it—if every time you looked into my eyes you saw me hanging from the end of a noose I had created for myself, how would you feel?" I shoved him back and he flinched at the contact, his breathing coming hard and fast, his glowing eyes narrowing.

I didn't give him time to answer me, "Would you want me to feel like that?" I paused, and said more calmly, my voice breaking, "Kade," I started, and at the sound of his own name, soft and broken coming from my lips his fire went out all at once and his jaw tensed, "Would you blame me at all for what I had done?"

He came and wrapped me in his arms, and I buried my face into his chest, "You have *nothing* to feel remorse about. *Nothing*. Do you understand me?"

He nodded against my hair, "I do," he said.

Ricon's face came to the forefront of my mind, smiling wickedly, his eyes alight with insanity. He would pay for what he'd done to us that day. I would make sure of it before the end.

Alaric cleared his throat, "Welcome back brother," he said, "We were wondering when you'd snap out of it."

"Asses, the lot of you," Kade grumbled, but a small smile lit his eyes and I wanted to cry at the sight. I stood on tip-toe to kiss his still Grace-warmed cheek.

"I've missed you."

He bowed his head low to nuzzle his forehead against mine, "I missed you, too. I'm sorry."

"Don't be."

"Liana," Finn called, and I turned slightly to see him standing near the water, his boots on the shore and his trousers rolled up to his ankles. "They're coming," he said, pointing out into the black water rippling with ribbons of shimmering silvery blue.

He was right, though I saw only three of them streaking their way through the water, just under the opaque surface.

Kade planted a soft kiss on my forehead and spun me around, "Go," he said, giving me a little shove and a tap on my rear.

I gasped at the vulgarity of the action but rather enjoyed it. I made my way over to Finn, kicking my boots off as I went.

Alaric, Tiernan, and Kade stepped up closer to the water. They didn't visibly ready themselves for an assault as they had the last time, but if you knew them at all, you would know they were always ready for an attack. Poised. Their muscles taught and eyes always searching their surroundings. Looking for danger, filing away ways to escape, measuring distances, and noting changes as they occurred.

I took Finn's outstretched hand and together we stepped in the water to meet the Wraiths.

CHAPTER EIGHT

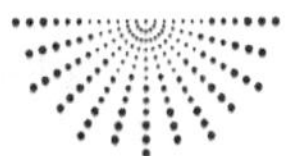

LIANA

I had been right—there were only three. Their movements slow, and a bit disjointed compared to their perfect formation three nights before. They halted several yards from where we stood, now up to our knees in the icy water. They raised their heads from the surface and stared at us with unblinking black eyes.

The one in front—who I assumed was leading the other two, was not the same Wraith we'd spoken to before. Though they mostly looked identical, I could tell this one was different.

"What news?" I asked of the Wraith, "Where are the others?"

I noticed the way the one in front swam. It was having trouble holding itself up. And I heard it hissing with the effort.

"Is everything alright?" Finn asked.

...the boats come...the boats leave Emeris...they come here...

I swallowed, my face heating and fingers prickling with ice. A shiver darted up my spine, and Finn's gaze met mine, his jaw clenched. He had been right. The Mad King planned to bring an army form Emeris, but...

"How many?" I asked the Wraith who was shaking with the effort of staying afloat.

...there are many...we help queen...we sink two ships...

I shook my head, not understanding. How many is *many?*

I didn't ask them to fight, but they had anyway. And if they took down two ships, then how many could remain? Depending on the ship size, a warship could carry anywhere from three-hundred to five-hundred.

"How many ships?" Finn asked, his hand tightening around mine, the cold seeping through.

The Wraith shook its head, and closed its eyes, bowing its head. An image flashed into my mind. Finn gasped, staggering back. They were showing him, too.

I saw through the eyes of the Wraith. A fleet of ships above. Their hulls looked like dark shadows on the surface of the water. There were so many. As far as I could see, ships dotted the oceans surface. Twenty? Thirty? I couldn't tell.

Up to the surface she went, following the alpha Wraith, ready to attack, a long crystal-tipped spear in her hands. She broke the surface. It was chaos. There was fire, and ice, and shadow, and lightning. Arrows sailed through the dawning sky, finding their marks in silvery blue flesh.

Thousands. I was looking at an army of at least ten-thousand. I couldn't breathe—my chest tightened painfully, and I fell to my knees in the water. "Stop," I said between panting breaths, "Stop!"

All at once the images—the *memory* left my mind and I was thrown back into the present, sputtering and unable to catch my breath. My males surrounded me, trying to help me stand.

"What did it do?" Kade growled, and the Wraiths backed away.

"No, wait!" I called to them, and they halted.

Finn was utterly silent, still standing, his eyes were wide. He didn't look like he was breathing. "Finn," I called to him, and he snapped out of the trance-like state.

"Did you see?" he asked me, the weight of what stood against us tainting every word.

I nodded, and turned back to the Wraiths, extricating myself from the others. "I'm alright," I told them, "I just need a minute."

I could hardly make sense of the images still flooding my mind. There were Fae on the ships—though few. And Draconians in the sky—though not more than one hundred.

The bulk of the Mad King's army was made up of men. But not mortal men. They bore strange markings on their heads. A circle within a triangle within another circle. Alchemists. They cast incantations at them, poured potions into the sea. And all around the Wraiths fell, eyes wide in their final moments as they sunk down into the dark.

But how? How had Ricon got them to join his regime? The Alchemists were the ruling race of Emeris. They took power over the Vocari and the Endurans only a century past. Why would they leave themselves vulnerable to an attack on their own lands by sending their army here?

It doesn't matter, I thought. *They are coming. Ready or not.*

Even though the Wraiths sank two of their ships, Ricon's army was still ten-thousand strong. We had no hope of defeating them. The Horde armies totalled five-thousand men. They would outnumber us two to one.

...they will meet land soon... two moons... they make for the north... for the Wastes...

"What is it?" Alaric asked, and I turned to him in a daze.

I shook my head. Not able to bring myself to reiterate what I'd seen. His eyes were narrowed and focused, filled with latent worry. His hands were fists at his sides.

I looked to Finn, who still hadn't moved. For once he didn't look like he was trying to solve the problem. And that made it so much worse—more *real.*

"Finn," I said, and he lifted his head, "Tell them what we saw. I need to help her." I gestured to the Wraith who was sinking lower into the water. Catching a glimpse of a spot on the side of her neck that looked black—as though it'd been charred. They lost four of their pack. And many, *many* others from what we saw.

I couldn't help them all, but I would help this one. She didn't have to come back. She wasn't the one who struck the bargain—that was their alpha. But she did anyway. And that was honorable.

My males didn't try to stop me as I waded further into the water. The trio of Wraiths hissed at first, recoiling in fear.

"I won't hurt you. I want to help. I can heal you," I said to the one who was the most hurt—their new leader. "Please—let me help you." My heart broke at the sight of them. Afraid. Grieving.

Tears stung my eyes. It was what would become of us if we didn't think of a way to stop them. My court would fall. Families would lose loved ones. It would leave us broken and bleeding when he was through with us.

No. I would find a way. *We* would find a way.

"Please," I repeated, standing near the edge of the underwater embankment.

The Wraith came closer, it's glowing blue skin shimmering dully beneath the cold, dark water. Its movements were jerking—hesitant, but it came near, and I bent low so I was at eye level with the strange, beautiful creature.

Its black eyes were eerie but also so large and round they reminded me of a doe's. Innocent and frail. Its long silvery hair pooled around its sharp face in the water.

...not hurt us...

I shook my head, and reached out an arm, feeling the slick, silk-like topside of one of her tentacles. She recoiled slightly, but then relaxed.

The healing Grace was still one of the more difficult to wield. And now that I didn't have Aisling to help me anymore, it was hit or miss when I tried to use it. But this time it answered my call within seconds as though the Grace itself *knew* this was no practice run.

I flinched, finding not one, but seven dark spots within the Wraith. Seven grave injuries. It was a wonder the creature was even still alive. I heaved in a deep, quick breath and pushed—letting the Grace flow from me into the Wraith. Let the healing light wrap around the darkness, eat it away. Smother it.

But I had to keep pushing—keep calling forth the Grace to heal all of her wounds. My strength waned, and it became more difficult. My muscles tensed, my lungs ached, and my head throbbed. The last of the dark spots faded and I let go, falling back, my head heavier than I'd ever felt it.

The Wraith reached out to steady me, and I tried to refocus my gaze and find her face in the crooked, spinning world. My heart sputtered, trying to find its proper rhythm.

...you are strong... but you cannot defeat him... not alone...

Vaguely, I heard my guardians arguing behind us. I didn't have long before they saw how much trouble I had standing on my own and dragged me away.

"How?" I asked the creature, and she pulled me close.

An intense sadness drew down her eyes and mouth, her thin slimy fingers squeezed where they held my arms, imploring me to listen.

...queen must run...

CHAPTER NINE

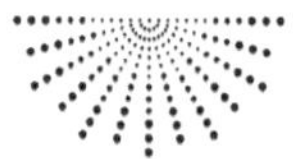

ALARIC

J couldn't believe it. Not when Finn told me, or when Liana confirmed it. Ten-thousand men. *Alchemists*. We knew a fair amount about their kind, but not nearly enough. Like us, there were some who were granted more strength than others, though for them it was more to do with natural selection than it was to do with the circumstances of their birth.

But we didn't know how many were gifted with the ability to use the ancient magical art and how many weren't. The army could be made up of foot soldiers, men not gifted by the power of the Alchemists, or they could *all* be gifted—though that was highly unlikely.

Damnit. I slammed a clenched fist down on the wide wooden desk. My dark chamber was only making the foreboding feeling worse than it already was. The walls seemed like they were closing in, the darkness growing claws.

Ten-thousand.

It didn't matter—gifted or not, were didn't have the army to match them.

Think, Alaric. Think!

There had to be a solution. There always was, wasn't there? So, why couldn't I see it…

We would have to kill the Mad King. It was the only way—cut off the head of the beast and the whole thing will fall. But that was if we found him. If we could get to him. And if we could somehow defeat him. There were too many *ifs*.

The council wasn't any help either. When Liana told them the size of the Mad King's army and that they would land by this night on the northwestern shores of the Wastes, there'd been silence. I thought none of them had taken the situation seriously until war was upon their doorstep.

And their answer… to send an *envoy*.

I sighed. As though the Mad King would be coaxed into discussing terms. Or as if he were interested in finding a *peaceful solution*. He didn't bring an army here to discuss terms—*no*, he meant to take back the throne and kill anyone who stands in his way… like Liana.

A pang in my chest almost had me doubling over.

I couldn't let him hurt her, and I couldn't let her give herself up to save others. I knew she was thinking it already—I'd seen it in her eyes and in the way she nodded and spoke so, *so* calmly. As if she were in a dream, or a nightmare and would soon wake. She hadn't been *there* since the Wraith showed her what made for the shores of her kingdom. She was a ghost of her regular self. As if she'd already given herself up.

I shook off the tremors coursing through my fingers and stood, needing to be mobile. She *had* to know—Ricon wouldn't settle for her life. The noble families who fought against him and their chil-dren—and their *children's children* would be made to pay for casting him out. He would kill half the Night Court and the other half would live in a state of perpetual fear and misery under his reign.

Save her. Save Liana and save as many of them as I can, it was all I could think. The only thing to do. But it was a foolish thought. Liana would never leave—and I'd never ask her to. It was why I loved her. It was her strength, her courage, her stubbornness, and her sense of duty. All those things that made her *her*.

The best I could do would be to die at her side. And it would be an honor.

I was meant to be resting, but how they expected me to rest was beyond my comprehension to understand. Kade and Finn stayed with her this evening. They were better at being in the moment—or at least Kade was. I hoped he was able to take her mind off it if only for a little while.

My thoughts scattered when I realized I was standing in front of Tiernan's door. I hardly remembered leaving my own chamber, never mind walking down the hall. I shook my head. Swallowed. Wondered if he was still awake, too.

The door was unlocked, and I turned the cool brass knob and swung it open as quietly as I could.

"Oh, Tiernan, I thought you would be asleep." I found him bent over a table pushed against the wall, his golden hair falling to cover his face. His hand hovered over the parchment, the quill wet with ink.

His green eyes shone in the lamplight, widening in surprise, "Alaric, I didn't expect—"

"What are you doing?"

I stepped in his chamber and closed the door behind me, taking a deep breath of the clean, crisp air flowing in through his window. Arrow cooed at me, ruffling his feathers before the creature flow off —likely to go keep a beady black eye on Liana.

"I had planned to ask you first, I swear."

My brows narrowed, "Ask me what? What are you writing, Tiernan? Who is that for?"

But before he answered I saw the seal set down next to the letter. Carved with the emblem of the Queen of the Day Court.

"You had better start talking." My hands clenched into fists of their own accord, and my breathing turned ragged and my skin, hot. What was he planning?

I felt fear in the room, and worry, and… and hope.

Chewing at the inside of my lip, I tried to calm myself. This was Tiernan. The Tiernan who saved Liana not once, but twice now. He loved her as I did—I'd felt it.

He was one of us.

"We need help, Alaric."

The meaning of what he was implying took a moment to unravel in my mind. "And you thought to ask the Day Court for aid? You know Queen Suriel is just as likely to put Liana's head on a pike and take her throne as the Mad King is!"

Tiernan held his hands up. Spoke very calmly, "The queen before the one who currently sits throne made it clear she wanted to reign over all of Meloran and that there should be only *one* court and only *one* way. Her way. But Suriel is not like her mother, just as Liana is unlike *her* mother."

"It's a fool's errand. Ricon's sights are not set on the throne of Day. What reason would they have to aid us? And regardless of what you might think, I am *telling* you, it isn't safe."

Tiernan squared his jaw—tossing his quill onto the table, "And who's to say he won't go after the Day Court next. We would stand a better chance united."

"Yes, but—"

"Honorem Copulare."

"What?"

Tiernan picked up the letter. Thrusted it into my hands, "Honorem Copulare. If Queen Suriel agrees to the meeting, no harm can come to Liana."

There, scrawled along the bottom of the parchment in large script read the words he spoke, *Honorem Copulare.* The ancient law of honor. If Liana requests a meeting under the law of honor and Suriel accepts—neither queen can harm the other.

"Suriel is an honorable queen. If she accepts the request for council, she will hold to her word. Liana will be safe." He sighed, falling onto his blanket-strewn bed, "What else can we do?" he asked.

I had no answer to give.

CHAPTER TEN

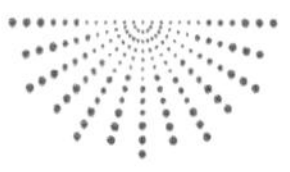

LIANA

The envoy left at dawn. I watched the three council-appointed riders gallop north until they passed from view. I didn't dare hope for a peaceful resolution to any of this. I could only hope for their safe and swift return. We all knew it was a waste of time—that the Mad King would turn them away the moment he laid eyes on their Night Court banners.

It was hopeless.

"The Queen of the Day Court will answer our call," Tiernan said, standing resolute at the window, staring out into the chilly autumn day. It had been two days since we'd sent Arrow with the message for Queen Suriel. He should have returned by now.

Finn left an hour before to deliver my order to Silas to place a legion at the border to the Wastes and evacuate all the northern villages. In the ridge of mountains separating my lands from those of my ancestors was only one place where an army could get through. The Galrûn Gap. At least, in that regard, we were lucky—knowing where he would march his army.

"You don't know that," I answered Tiernan, shrugging off Kade's attempt to rub more warmth into my shoulders and melt the crust of ice that kept forming over my skin like a shell.

My fingernails bit down into the palms of my hands, leaving half-moon indents when I finally released them. I agreed to sign the letter and send it with Arrow to the Day Court because it would've been foolish not to try *anything* we could. But did I believe Suriel would honor the ancient tradition of Honorem Copulare? No, not at all.

The waiting was the worst. With the Horde armies ready and waiting at the border, the northern villages evacuated, and every smith in the Night Court working around the clock to make swords and shields and arrowheads, we'd done all that was within our power for now.

It would take weeks for Ricon to march his army as far as the Galrûn Gap over land. All we could do was wait. Outnumbered as we were, taking the fight to them wasn't an option, but…

"I still say we find a way to kill Ricon," I blurted, "If giving myself up isn't an option," I said, cutting a glare to Alaric, "Then we *must* find another way to stop this war from happening. We can't win it, and I won't watch my court fall."

I felt Kade's sharp intake of breath at my back, "It isn't possible, Liana. With an army of ten-thousand and a legion of Dracs in the air, we'd never reach him."

I knew they were right, but that didn't make it any easier to accept. I wasn't even sure I could handle taking him on. After I healed the Wraith, I'd been all but drained—near collapse. The amount of power I'd need to harness to defeat him could destroy me. I hadn't had enough time to strengthen myself against the toll of my Graces. I spent nearly all my time using at least one of my Graces lately, if only to do just that—but was it too late?

How much time did we have?

I shivered and Kade tucked me into his chest. "It'll be alright. We'll find a way," he whispered, and I wished my Kade would come back. The Kade who laughed and joked and infuriated me to no end. I missed him.

I missed me, too.

We heard Arrow before we saw him. A screech penetrating the

room. Our heads turned all at once to the window just as the falcon came to land, not on the sill, but on the low coffee table inside. Right in front of me.

Tied above his left talon was a small scroll, sealed with the royal emblem. My stomach jumped into my throat. Arrow cawed, watching me with cool black eyes. Tiernan stepped in to retrieve the scroll, but Arrow backed away, moving to peck at his master's fingers.

Tiernan rolled his eyes at the creature, backing away, "The scroll is meant for you, Liana. Arrow never fails a delivery." He threw the falcon a look halfway between pride and annoyance.

"So, *now* you'll let me touch you?" I asked the bird, moving from the warmth of Kade's lap to kneel before the low table. Arrow hopped to the edge, moving his small head this way and that— getting a good look at me. Measuring.

I shook my head, "Alright then."

I reached out and took hold of the small scroll, gently untying the waxen strings securing it in place. My fingers brushed the tiny soft feathers on the falcon's legs and he bristled, jumping back the second I freed the scroll from his body.

"Thank you," I said to him, and hopped to the edge of the table and flew out the open window. "Not a very trusting creature, is he?" I asked Tiernan, breaking the royal seal.

He shook his head, coming to sit on the edge of the table.

I licked my lips, unsure what I wished for the scroll to contain. Should I *want* the queen of day to accept my request for council? I would be lying if I said I didn't always dream of seeing the lands to the south for myself. The pristine beaches, the lush forests, and the land that seemed forever trapped in perpetual summer. But…

"Would you open the damned thing, already?" Alaric said, running a fisted hand through his dark hair.

Sighing, I unrolled the scroll, pressing it flat against the table so we could all see. The three males leaned in.

I gasped. The message from the queen of day was clear. Simple. Making it more difficult to discern her intent.

My court awaits your arrival.
Honorem Copulare.

"We need to make ready," Alaric said. "We need to notify the council, and not all of us can go with you. At least one of us will need to remain behind. There are still those within *these* palace walls who would seek to unseat you."

Kade stood, "How do you even know she will honor the request for council? The right of Honorem Copulare hasn't been invoked in millennia."

Tiernan cocked his head at the Draconian, "There's been no need for it—"

"So, are *you* willing to guarantee her safety?"

Kade's eyes sparked to life. His Grace ignited. Alaric gave him a warning glance, "We have no other choice—"

"And I suppose you would have *me* stay behind. I can see it already. Tiernan knows the lands and you'll need Finn's mind. And *you*. You would never allow her to go without you."

Kade was right but arguing about it would solve nothing. We had to take the chance. I didn't like the idea of leaving Kade behind any more than I was sure he liked the idea of letting me go without him. But there was one way we could still keep watch over one another.

It was time. Full moon or not.

We may not get another chance.

"Stop it, all of you," I said in a rush, standing on leaden legs, "We *will* go to the Day Court and ask for their aid. Alaric is right, we have no other choice but to trust they'll honor the old law," I nodded to my captain, "And someone will need to stay behind and keep an eye on things here... but first we'll be bonded."

Kade narrowed his glowing yellow gaze at me, "But I thought Finn said—"

"I *know* what Finn said. But we don't have time to wait for the full moon. I won't leave you here without having a way to watch over you."

The Draconian nodded his understanding. He'd go mad if he didn't have some way of knowing I was alright, too. "We bond then."

Tiernan and Alaric nodded their agreement. "Call a council meeting and tell Finn when he returns that the bonding ceremony will happen *tonight*. We'll leave for the Day Court tomorrow at first light."

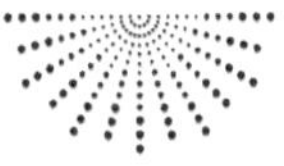

CHAPTER ELEVEN

I still couldn't believe Edris convinced me to allow him to come with us. I shook my head. The council had been against the idea of going to the Day Court, even with the other queen's promise of honor to protect me. But Silas and the nobles of the royal council saw our options were few and combining our forces with those of the Day Court would give us a better chance.

A week, they'd said. We had a week to get there, get an answer, and return. Or they'd be forced to take certain 'measures'. We were right to decide to leave Kade behind, especially with Edris now accompanying us. There were few at the palace who we could trust fully. Silas was trustworthy, but when we left for the south in the morning, he would leave for the north, to continue evacuating villages and forming lines at the border.

"Thank you, Jaen," I said for the third time, "Truly, I don't know how I'd have done this without your help."

She'd helped me light upwards of a hundred candles. Her with a long wooden stick, and me with nothing more than the touch of a finger and the will of my Grace. The parlor looked ethereal bathed in orange light, the middle of the floor cleared of furniture to allow space for the ceremony to take place. With hardly a wisp of breeze in the air tonight, the room was warm and smelled of burning sage and spice.

My hair was pulled back in an intricate knot, courtesy of the young servant as well. I wore a dress Darius altered to fit me only an hour before. Black silk with lace at the neckline, trailing florals and swirls down my arms. It felt lighter than air and softer than anything I'd ever touched. The tailor had been saving it, he'd said, for a special occasion.

I couldn't tell him why I needed it in such a hurry, but something told me the ancient male already knew. Wise and cunning as he was. I was sure nothing escaped his notice.

"Of course, Your Majesty," Jaen replied, finishing up with the last few candles. "And thank you—for trusting me."

I heard Aisling in her voice. Could almost see my healer friend behind her eyes. In another life Jaen and I could've been friends. I nodded to her. "What do you think of all this?"

She scrunched up her face at me, seemingly perplexed at the question, or rather, that I would ask her opinion at all.

"A bond is a very sacred thing," she said carefully, "It's not called the Immortal Bond because it is a bond between two immortal beings. It's called that because it lasts forever—for as long as you both—er—you *five* shall live."

My lips pursed, and I bit the inside of my cheek.

"I have seen you with them, Majesty. I know how you love them —and I know why you would seek to forge a bond with each. For the love you share, but for reasons more—" she stumbled, trying to find the right word.

"More practical."

"Yes, exactly."

"So, you don't think it's wrong to bond to more than one mate?"

She sighed, considering my question. Shook her head, "I believe it's entirely possible to love more than one person… so, then I don't see why it would be wrong to bind yourself to *all* of the males you love. It would be more wrong to choose one and forsake the others? Wouldn't you agree?"

I smiled, nodding, feeling nothing but sincerity rolling off her in waves. "Thank you."

"You have to stop doing that."

I cocked my head at her.

"Thanking me," she explained, laughing while she straightened the decanter and glasses on the table by the wall, "I'm only doing my job."

Right. I blew out a breath, licking my suddenly dry lips.

"I suppose we should let them come in now," I said, trailing off.

They would be restless by now, cooped up in the dining room. But they understood. I didn't like that we had to rush this of all things, but since that was the way it had to be, I wanted it be as perfect as possible.

You only bond once after all—even if that bonding is a bond made between four males and one female.

We'd have to be very precise, perfect in our wording and timing, but Finn was confident it would work. And so was I.

If I was right, Morgana had bound herself to her not four, but *five* Draconian guardians. And if they could do it, so could we.

"Would you like me to go and get them, majesty?" Jaen asked, folding her hands neatly at her front, an encouraging smile tugging at the corners of her mouth.

"No," I said, my pulse pounding in my ears, "I'll get them."

"Then I'll take my leave. Good luck, Liana."

Deep breaths. *That's it.* In and out.

I swallowed, fidgeting with the delicate fabric of my gown, and made for the dining room.

The hallways were dark, and much cooler than the parlor. I rushed through them to get to my males, anxious—no, *eager* to see them and to do what we should have done long ago. There was no reason to be nervous, I told myself. Despite my fear of what others might think, I knew in my bones this was the right way for me. For *us.*

I wanted nothing more than to be joined in every possible way to them. And if we were to meet our ends when Ricon set his army upon us, then at least we'd have this one thing. And if there was an afterlife, perhaps we'd be together there, too. Through the strength of our Immortal Bonds.

Exhaling, I rolled my shoulders back, set my jaw and strolled into the dimly lit chamber. They sat in silence. My four *perfect* warriors. Alaric, with his head bent—deep in thought. Kade, pacing the floor, looking more nervous than I thought him capable of. Tiernan, standing quietly with Arrow at the window, absently stroking the falcon's feathers. And Finn, nodding as though reassuring himself that this would work—that it was the right thing.

Kade was the first to notice me, and stopped mid-stride, his jaw dropping. He took a moment to school his features, shut his maw, and take a breath. The others raised their eyes to meet mine one by one. Their stares caressed me from tip to toe, awakening the embers at my core into a slow-burning flame.

"It's time," I said, not trusting myself to say more than two words.

Finn and Alaric rose, and the four of them came to me. Alaric brushed the lace sleeve of my gown and his emotions ran through me like lightning's strike. Pain, desire, trust, fear, and *love*. I felt the emotions from all my males. Recognized their mirror images within me.

Tiernan clasped my hand in his, and Finn tucked a stay hair back into the knot at the nape of my neck.

Kade took my other hand, "We're ready," he said, "Lead the way."

I led them down the hallway and into the orange glow of the parlor.

"You've outdone yourself," Finn said, his eyes roving the large room.

I shrugged, "I just want this to be perfect."

"And it is perfect," Tiernan injected.

A hot blush climbed up my neck and I reached for the decanter, ready to pour us all a drink.

"Allow me," Alaric said, taking it from me, his hands brushing against mine. I shivered at the contact, my stomach tightening at the thought of having him again. At having all of them.

Tonight, I would have Kade. I looked to where the mighty Draconian warrior sat, pensive, chewing his bottom lip. Since he would be the one to stay behind—we'd have to consummate our bond before myself and the others left at first light. I licked my lips.

I'd wanted Kade since the moment I saw him. His strong jaw, chiseled chest, bronze skin, and beautiful black wings. But now that I knew him, I wanted him even more—and in different ways. My protector. My friend. The male who would do anything for those he cares about without a thought towards his own wellbeing. The stubborn ass who isn't afraid to speak his mind. I love all of him.

I just wished he would look at me. He was so damned quiet over there, I was beginning to think he was having seconds thoughts.

Don't be ridiculous, Liana. He wants this just as much as you. He's nervous, that's all.

Alaric passed around the chalices and raised his own, "To Liana," he said.

"To us," I corrected.

"To us," the others intoned, and we all drained our chalices of wine.

Alaric set his down and turned to Finn, "We're ready. Show us how it should be done."

The Draconian nodded and turned toward the empty circle of floor in the room's middle. We followed.

My heart beat erratically against my ribcage, and my palms slicked with sweat.

Finn led me to the center where the moonlight could reach me from the open terrace. The chill breeze shocked my sweat-dampened skin.

"The ritual requires contact, so we all must touch her." Finn took told of my hand, gave a reassuring squeeze and a nod. He whispered only for me, "It's alright. It's going to work."

And he was right—I *was* worried about it not working, or somehow only binding me to one of them instead of all of them. But there was a small part of my mind that rebelled, telling me this wasn't fair to them.

The Immortal Bond cannot be undone.

If it worked, they would be tied to me forever. Never able to have families of their own. I was depriving them of normal lives.

Alaric took my other hand, and my breathing hitched at the contact. Tiernan gently circled my wrist, above where Finn still clasped my hand. Kade did the same on the other side.

My breathing sped up—becoming more ragged. Panicked.

"Wait," I said, but didn't pull away. I swallowed, "Are—are you all certain this is what you want?"

There wasn't a trace of doubt or weakness in any of their eyes. They regarded me with unwavering strength, certainty, and devotion. As one, they said, "Yes."

"And you?" Alaric said, faltering, averting his gaze, "Are *you* certain?"

Looking at him—at all my males, I realized I had never been more certain of anything in my entire life. They might've been the *only* thing I was certain of.

"I've never been more certain of anything."

Alaric snapped his head up at my response. His jaw tightened.

"Let's do this," Kade said, and I felt the place where his hand gripped my arm warm with the activation of his Grace.

I nodded my agreement. "What now, Finn?"

"Do you all remember the words?"

"Yes," Tiernan said, and the rest of us nodded. The ancient words were few—only six words in the tongue of old, spoken with intent and while bound of flesh—would bind us of heart and mind forever.

Finn knelt, and with a piece of chalk pulled from his trousers, he drew on the floor at my feet. It was an intricate pattern of lines and swirls and knots. A sigil?

He saw the questioning look I gave him when he rose, and he squeezed my hand again, blushing, "It's a sigil of the Alchemists," he said with a bit of distaste in his tone, "I'd prefer not to use it, but this particular one strengthens the potency of an incantation. I thought —well it can't hurt, right?"

The corner of my mouth turned up in a smirk, "So prepared," I teased him.

He smiled back, "All you have to do is say the words, Liana. Only once, but with intent to bind with all four of us."

My teeth clenched, and my grip on Alaric's and Finn's hands tightened.

"It'll be alright," Alaric breathed, "Just close your eyes and focus."

I blew out a long breath, letting my eyes fall closed. I *felt* them. Kade's hot touch, Tiernan's deft fingers, Finn's cool palm against mine, and Alaric's strong grip.

Their emotions assaulted me in a barrage of passion, love, and anxiety. At first, I tried to block them out, but once I let go—let their emotions run through me, and mine through them, it was easier. Calmer. As though we were already one.

You can do this, Liana, I told myself. *I* will *bind to all my males.*

I licked my lips, and swallowed, readying myself to speak the six most powerful words I'd ever speak. Before I'd even uttered the first words, I felt the raw, ancient magic of the gods building behind my breastbone.

I pictured them all in my minds eye, felt the connections between our flesh. And then I said in as strong and sure of a voice as I could muster, "Adîra eis, et aeterna promnîn falrún."

My skin tingled. My head emptied. And my chest broke out in a thin layer of cold sweat.

"Now, quickly, we say it as one!" Finn said.

And together, with one united voice, my males made their solemn vow, "Adîra eis, et aeterna promnîn falrún."

My heart jolted as though struck by lightning. A violent wind tore through the room, billowing the curtains and extinguishing the flames. I gasped, trying to catch my breath as though it was the first one I'd ever taken and I'd forgotten how to do it.

I opened my eyes and saw… me. Standing there in a black dress, looking back at myself as though staring at a reflection. I blinked and was staring at my males. They were smiling, their expressions varied from excitement to incredulity.

"Can you feel it?" asked Tiernan, his wide smile shining in the moonlight.

"It worked," Finn sighed, looking close to tears at our triumph.

Alaric released my hand, and the others followed suit. Unsteady on my feet, I swayed, and then righted myself, leaning against the back of a chair.

Could I feel it? I wasn't sure.

"What does it feel like?" I asked, my brows pulling together.

Before any of my males could answer, I felt it. A pull. Like a tether. It tugged insistently though gently at my chest. And if I concentrated… yes! There was more than one tether, and each had a different texture to it. I couldn't have explained it, but I *knew* which tether belonged to each of my males, and I could… I could go across the tethers—to feel them. To see through their eyes as I had accidently done only a moment before.

"Wait—I feel it!" My heart ached in the most glorious way, and my cheeks hurt from the strength of my smile. I laughed, the sound bubbled up from within me as though it were more of an eruption.

"I can't believe it worked," Kade said through his own fits of laughter.

Finn put a hand to his chest in mock agony, "You hurt me, brother, saying such things."

"Oh, come on, you didn't think it would work either," Alaric chastised, his eyes alight like I hadn't seen them do it so long.

Finn shook his head, "No, I knew it would work."

Tiernan, as though oblivious to anything they were saying, came to where I stood, his jade green gaze never once faltering. He lifted my hand from my side and pressed his warm lips against the back. A shock ran through me at the touch of his lips. My body recognizing part of its soul within him. The split pieces aching to rejoin.

"Forever," he said, his gaze burning into me.

I nodded, running a finger down his sharp, smooth jaw, "Forever."

CHAPTER TWELVE

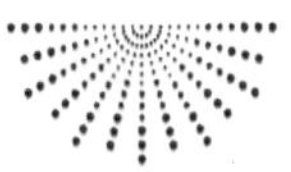

KADE

She looked like the night incarnate standing there in her midnight black dress with a half moon smile. I didn't deserve her—could never deserve her, and yet she was mine and I hers. Alaric poured the second round of drinks and Finn nodded to our captain, accepting his chalice with a small salute.

The pull of the Immortal Bond was unmistakable. Like there was a rope tied to her at one end and tied to me at the other. But the rope wasn't a restraint. The tie wasn't unwelcome.

Despite myself, I felt... excited. When Alaric passed me a filled chalice, I tipped the contents back, letting the cool spirits burn their way down my throat and settle in my gut like warm honey.

Tiernan stepped away from Liana and her eyes locked onto mine. Her smiled faltered, and a flush rose to her cheeks. I'm not sure what she did, but the pull behind my ribcage intensified— reeling me into her. She called through the bond and it forced me to answer. The rope taut between us. The air electrified.

She bit her bottom lip and the weight of her stare deepened.

My cock twitched.

I swallowed, meaning to walk over to her, but finding myself nearly sprinting to close the gap.

"What did you do?" I accused her, glaring at my feet like they'd done something without my permission.

She blinked, her lips parted, and shook her head. A strand of her silvery hair came loose, and I itched to touch it, "I—I don't know," she laughed nervously—the sound doing all kinds of welcome, and *unwelcome* things to my body. "I just wanted you to come here."

I pursed my lips, "Well, it worked. You've summoned me," I teased, leaning in. An image of her run through with my blade flashed before my eyes before I could kiss her neck. My stomach turned and it snuffed the flames in my core out.

"Don't do that," she said, and grabbed my arm with a surprisingly strong grip. "Don't pull away from me."

"I'm sorry," I shrugged, and let out a rough breath, shaking off the tension in my wings.

She shook her head at me, "I will have you, Kade. *All* of you. And then maybe you'll finally stop thinking you aren't worth it."

The fire that had died a moment before roared back into chaotic flame. Her eyes glowed violet, and I watched the color turn to a molten russet gold—not unlike the glow of Draconian eyes. I'd never seen them that color before.

My muscles tightened. It was the plan—for us to *consummate* the bond tonight. To strengthen it before she left with the others at dawn. And I wanted her. *Gods,* I wanted her. I'd wanted her from the moment I first saw her—still pale from the long sea voyage, her icy blue eyes coy and defiant. But, after everything…

I tried to weigh my next words, "But I still haven't beaten you at chess. Wasn't that the deal?"

She narrowed her eyes at me, "Fine," she said, chin lifted, and shoulders pushed back, "Then we play—for as long as it takes."

"You can't let me win."

She scrunched her brows, crossed her lace-covered arms. Nodded. "And you can't throw the game."

"Agreed."

She clucked her tongue, "Always so difficult. Stubborn as a mule."

I could help it, I smiled at her, shaking my head, "I'll never be more stubborn than you."

"Come have a drink!" Alaric hollered, beckoning us over.

"Tonight, we celebrate," Finn said, knocking his chalice against Tiernan's.

They were right. We only had so many days and nights left before Ricon's armies would come to fight for Liana's throne. Tonight, we'd celebrate. And I'd do everything I could to give Liana what she wanted.

Tomorrow we'd ready for war.

I ROLLED the strong spirits around on my tongue, considering her remaining pieces and mine—trying to find the best move.

Practicing with Finn and Tiernan had paid off. She'd beaten me twice already, but even she admitted they were hard-won victories. But this time, I had her. Or at least, I was pretty sure I did.

I swallowed the spirits, setting my third empty chalice down on the low table between us. The fire blazed in the hearth next to us, keeping the room warm and bathed in just enough light to see by. I couldn't say how much time had passed. Hours, surely, but she showed no signs of giving in or stopping. Her delicate face set with stubborn determination. It was so severe at times I almost laughed.

But I couldn't. I respected her too much. So like me—like Alaric. Like all of us, really. We didn't give up easily and neither would she.

Liana wreaked of desire, the scent strong and cloying—seeping through her and into my pores.

She had her mind set on having me, and that thought, combined with her scent drove me almost to madness trying to keep my mind from rebelling against the idea and my hands from wanting to reach out and grab her. Take her right there on the floor.

Patience was not my forte. But we had a deal. And I intended to honor it either way.

I moved my piece, seeing the only two options she had for her own turn. One might save her. The other would condemn her, and if I did it right—she wouldn't even realize until it was too late.

She looked at the board, her eyes widened, throwing me a cutting glance before she went back to studying the pieces.

Her hand hovered over the piece that could save her, and I held my breath. She swallowed. Was she worried? She looked worried. Or was it more excitement I saw shining in her eyes?

At the last moment, she changed her mind and took up the piece that would spell her doom. Moved it. Placed it.

I beamed.

Almost immediately, she realized what she had done and gasped. "But—" she started but didn't finish.

One last move and I'd win. After so many games I'd lost. And then she'd get what she wanted.

A slow, sexy smile spread over her lips, she caught the bottom one between her teeth. Her eyes burned.

Shit.

She knew I had won. There was nowhere she could move her king where I couldn't get to it.

"You did it," she breathed, her hands curling into the silky black fabric of her dress.

I lifted the bishop, but before I could place it, the board flew from the table—crashing into the hearth, the pieces scattering onto the floor—into the flames.

She pounced over the table with a hunger in her expression like I'd never seen on a female. The weight of her body pressed into me and my cock hardened at the slightest brush of her contact. I grunted as her lips came down onto mine. Hard. Insistent.

I stiffened, my body tightening. But then…

Then the shock wore off. The tether in my chest vibrated, and I wanted to roar at the force of it. I clamped my arms around her. Kissed her greedily, swallowing her sharp moans. Her hand brushed against my right wing and I shuddered, my Grace igniting like a column of fire down my spine.

I'd imagined this moment so many times. *Gods,* nothing had ever felt so damned *right*. Nothing else mattered. I couldn't think of anything but her. Her sweet smell. Her soft fiery touch. Her spicy spirit-spiked taste. She wanted me, and I wanted her. It was primal. Innate.

Beyond my control.

CHAPTER THIRTEEN

LIANA

I knew the moment he gave in to his desire. His body softened and then molded to me—hardening again. His hands grasped at my waist and his lips were fevered and frantic against mine. I could hardly breath. The *feel* of him. It was overtaking every one of my senses. The Immortal Bond making the connection stronger.

My heart fluttered in my chest like a leaf caught in a storm's wind. The fire at my core roiled at our contact—awakening into a violent blaze.

I couldn't touch enough of him. I wanted more. I pressed against him, settling into his lap. His impressive length nudged at my inner thigh and I convulsed at the sensation cascading over me. Kade groaned, and it was all I could do not to tear the clothes from his body.

My Grace pushed against me—the fire building into an almost painful pressure against my skin. Kade's Grace heated in response. Our lips parted for an instant and I saw the wild glowing of his eyes —how his breaths came in ragged pants through his parted lips.

This is dangerous, I thought.

He nodded.

Had he heard my thoughts?

Two fire-Graced Fae fucking...

He spoke the thought down through the tether connecting us, and I jolted at the sound of his deep timber resounding in my mind. Licked my lips.

He was right—we'd burn down the palace.

"We should leave," he said aloud, lifting me onto him in one swift movement.

"Hurry," I whispered against his lips before yanking them back to mine. He wrapped an arm around my middle and ran for the terrace. Cold wind whistled by my ears and my stomach dropped. When I opened my eyes again, we were flying through the ink-stained night.

"There!" I shouted moments later, unable to wait any longer. The wetness between my legs and the *aching* need in my gut needed to be satisfied. Now.

Kade nodded, lowering us onto the outcropping of rock below the cliff—only twenty yards above the crashing of the waves below. No trees or homes or palaces to burn. Just stone, water, and moonlight.

Our feet connected with the black rock, and I pushed him back —using all my strength to force him against the cliff wall. He smashed into it, shock registering in his features before I jumped back onto him, wrapping my legs securely around his waist. His cock pressed against my sex—only his trousers and my delicate silk panties standing in our way.

His hand wound up my back, grabbing a fistful of my hair, crushing my body to him.

I fumbled with the buttons on his trousers. He spun, pressing my back against the stone. The wind knocked from my lungs for a second before I could fill them again. Stars danced before my eyes.

He reached down between my breasts, his hands brushing against the swell of them—forcing my nipples to stand erect— aching. Down my stomach. Between my thighs. The fire simmered on the surface of my skin. I breathed hard and fast to calm it.

I need him.

I lifted my skirts for him, pulling them up high—bunching them in a fist.

I want him inside me.

He growled. Tore my panties from me.

I gave up with the buttons and ripped them from the fabric. His cock sprang free. Huge and dripping with his own burning desire.

His glowing eyes met mine and time seemed to slow. Our breaths puffed like steam in the chill autumn air… and then it sped up again. He lifted me, pressed me against the stone and thrust into me. I gasped at the fullness. At the slight pain that morphed into the most glorious pleasure. So—*so* full.

I clawed at his vest and tunic—tearing them from his body. Running my hands over the ridges and valleys of his scorching muscle. With each of his thrusts my back rammed against the stone. He wrapped his arms around my back, trying to absorb some of the impact. But it didn't hurt. Far from it.

His kiss became fevered, almost delirious. He caught my bottom lip between his teeth and I almost came undone.

Kade slowed his pace, and the heat at my core built. Our shared bond and our shared Grace were too much. He shuddered against me, his fingers digging into my back and mine scratching into his.

I moaned against his lips, "Kade," I whimpered, my body shaking as the quickening began deep within. Growing and growing with each quick thrust.

He sucked in a breath, and I let go. He cried out, finding his release with me, and we burst into magnificent, blazing flame…

CHAPTER FOURTEEN

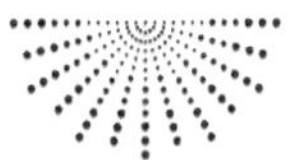

LIANA

"Are you sure you're alright to ride?" Alaric asked for the third time as he finished buckling the saddle onto my horse.

Its name was Scylla, and the stable-boy assured me she was the most docile horse he'd ever tended to.

I pet her long mane as she stooped to pick up another mouthful of hay. Chewed it with her enormous chomping teeth.

"I told you already. I'm fine."

Dawn had already broken over Meloran, dying the sky a soft, hazy, orange. We should have left already. It would be a long journey. We wouldn't reach the border until late in the evening, and then it would take us half a day still to make our way to the Day Queen's palace.

That was the stretch Alaric and the others most worried about. The bit between their border and the palace. We'd steer clear of villages and other Fae as much as we could. But it was also why we wore neutral colors. Nothing to give away our status or represent our court's colors of midnight blue and silver.

"He must've taken it easy on you," Finn teased, "Probably afraid you'd break."

I pouted, blushing in earnest. Tried to tie my bursting saddlebags to Scylla. Kade had left an hour earlier—to check the state of things with Silas and the Horde. He would return to the palace later this eve to keep an eye on things here, too. At the first sign of trouble, he'd send me a message through the bond and Finn would fly me home as quickly as he was able.

He'd already sent me a few messages—explaining what he'd do to me when I returned. I'd had to squash the birthing of fire at my core several times already that morning. But I was glad he'd finally come back to himself. I hoped his guilt and torment over what'd happened was finally over.

And I *was* sore. But I wasn't about to tell *them* that. My back, I'd healed—the roadmap of purple and black would've made for an uncomfortable ride. But I didn't heal the slight aching down below. That, I would leave to heal on its own.

"Here," Tiernan said, stepping in, "Let me help."

Groaning, I relinquished the bag to him, and he deftly secured it to one side of Scylla and lifted the other, securing it to her other side in a matter of seconds. "What's in these?" he asked, quirking a brow.

I lifted my chin and narrowed my eyes at him, "I'll need clothes, won't I?"

He had the audacity to roll his eyes at me—but only playfully. I was about to shove him when Arrow came screeching out of the clouds to land on his master's shoulder. The falcon followed Edris when he'd left the night before. He must be exhausted.

"Did he make it to the border?" Tiernan asked Arrow as though the bird could answer him and stroked the feathers on his breast. "Such a good falcon," he crooned. Arrow didn't seem miffed or distraught, so it was safe to assume Edris had made it safely to the border and Arrow didn't see the need to follow him anymore.

Edris would announce our coming to the Day Court and wait there for our arrival. Though he maintained a very serious front, my father seemed more than a little excited to be allowed to join us.

Enya had her reservations about the Day Court and never would have sought to repair the tear between our court and theirs.

But Edris was different. More like me. Eager to carve new paths and curious to discover new things. I had been wrong about him… and my males were right, he was the only wind-Graced noble at court. It would be idiotic of me not to take the chance to develop that Grace—even if it meant telling him the truth about my Graces and trusting him not to tell others.

Eventually, a time would come where my court would have to know—or they would find out. But that time hadn't come quite yet.

Arrow flew off Tiernan's shoulder and went to land on a tall post outside the stables, pruning himself in the warmth of the rising sun. "How long have you had him?"

Tiernan smirked, "A very long time. Sometimes I think the rodent might somehow be immortal, too. He's been with me nearly twenty years and was full-grown when I found him with a broken wing on my uncle's estate."

"He seems to fly well now. Did you mend it for him?"

"After he almost bit my fingers off, yes. I didn't know it at the time, but it wasn't only me helping Arrow to heal," he said, staring fondly at his companion, "He helped me, too. I was in a dark place then."

"What do you mea—"

"We should go," Finn called to us, leading his horse from the stable behind Alaric. "Dawn is breaking, and we have a long way to go."

"He's right," Tiernan said, looking away—his golden hair falling to shroud his face from me. "Here, let me help you up."

I let him lift me onto Scylla, and bless the beast, she didn't so much as budge. I sighed in relief.

"I'll lead you out. Just remember to grip the saddle with your thighs," he said with a wink, "Alaric means to set a cruel pace to make up for the time we lost this morning."

I groaned.

"Chin up, Liana," said Tiernan, "At least you aren't returning to a court you relinquished all ties to. Going to see a queen you used to guard while now guarding another."

A pang in my chest.

I hadn't thought of it—how Tiernan would be returning to his home court as a guest. The last communication he'd had with the Day Court was to inform them he wouldn't be returning. Queen Suriel never wrote him back. And as far as I knew he hadn't heard from his uncle either. They let him go without so much as a word to even try to make him stay.

I'd never have let him go so easily. I'd have chased him across oceans if I had to. What sort of people didn't know valiance and loyalty when they saw it? Who would toss it away so easily?

"I'm sorry," I said.

He shook his head, turning away to lead me out of the stables with a hand on Scylla's tackle. "It doesn't matter. I didn't belong there, and I think they all knew it."

I nodded. I knew what it was like to feel as though you didn't belong. It was how I felt most days in the palace. I belonged with my males—that I knew for certain. But I never got that sense of belonging I thought I'd find at court. I didn't settle into my role as queen as snuggly as I'd hoped. And I never would.

"I don't think you belong to a place," I mused, "You belong to the people in it."

He turned, stopping Scylla in her slow walk and smiled a close-lipped smile. A dimple in his cheek. The sunlight playing in his hair. "I belong to you," he said, laying a hand over his chest.

I felt the bond tugging at my core. "And I, you."

He turned back to continue leading me to where Alaric and Finn waited on the southern road. I got the feeling Tiernan has been waiting a long time to find someone worthy to belong to. Thank the goods that someone was me. I beamed feeling like the luckiest female ever to have been born.

"Hurry up!" Alaric called back to us.

I stuck my tongue out at the captain and his eyes widened at the childish gesture, "Last I checked, *I* was still the queen. Have a little patience!"

Tiernan snorted a laugh, leading me on a little more quickly than before.

My rear was numb by the time the sun set behind the trees. My thighs screaming and lower back aching. *Ugh.* After this trip, I'd never travel by horseback again.

At least the border was close, and we'd be making camp for the night soon. Soon I'd have a warm fire and a belly full of food. I salivated at the thought. I should have taken Edris' suggestion and traveled by carriage. It would have cost us another day, but I imagine I'd be much less sore and not have to expend my energy using my Grace to heal myself, so I could sleep without aching.

Finn brought up the rear and at my loudly exaggerated sigh, he spurred his steed faster to come up alongside me. "Are you alright?" he asked, giving me a pained smile.

I sighed again, "Please tell me we'll make camp soon."

He laughed, and I turned to meet his bright honey eyes. "We will. Just a bit further."

I'd been trying to distract myself. Occupying my thoughts with anything but the clomping of hooves and the tang of damp earth and dung. I wondered if Finn knew the answers to the questions rattling around in my brain.

I wondered if I'd need to *re*-consummate the bond between myself and Alaric. And if the consummation should happen before or after the actual ceremony to have the best effect... because that would mean I'd need to bed Tiernan again. I swallowed, soothing the ache of desire in my belly.

Really, I just wanted them again.

I knew it. Might as well admit it. Even though I still bore the soreness from Kade the night before.

And then there was Finn, too. He was the only one I hadn't had yet, and I wondered what it'd be like with him to share my bed. With the others, I knew what to expect, but I was at a loss with Finn. My quiet, thoughtful guardian. What would it be like when he…

"*Gods*, Liana. Your scent is driving me wild," he said, shaking his head.

Oops. "I forgot about the whole smelling desire thing. Sorry," I said, clucking my tongue, not sorry at all if I was being honest, "But we do need to consummate our bond. You're the only one that—"

"Not yet," he interrupted, giving his head a small shake—his eyes fixed on the road ahead.

"But I thought you said we should all—"

"I know, but—well—I don't want us to force it. I think it should happen… naturally. And I'll wait as long as that takes."

My brows knitted together, and I was sure I had the most confused expression on my face, "Forced?" I asked him. "Finn, do you think I don't want you?"

He watched where Alaric and Tiernan turned a bend in the narrow road up ahead, "It's not about that," he whispered, finally looking at me. "I want you, too." A sudden hunger set his iris' aglow and the gold chain he still wore around his neck glinted in the sun. "With you, it's different. I want it to be more than a means to an end. More than just fucking. I want you to want me in the moment because—well, because you simply *do*. Not because you feel compelled to follow through with your vow."

My throat went dry and my heart squeezed.

I could say nothing. Not after that. I gave him a nod and tugged at the tether binding us together to tell him I understood. And I would wait with bated breath for that moment, too. I calmed the roused emotions of lust and desire coursing through me with deep, steady breaths.

He sucked in a deep breath of his own, "Besides, you'll be needing a rest after my brother was through with you—am I right?"

"Ugh, Finn!"

He winked at me and sped off to catch up with the others, leaving me lashing at the reins, trying to spur Scylla to follow. But the damned beast wouldn't speed to anything more than a lazy canter.

I shook my head, giving up. Docile, *indeed.*

CHAPTER FIFTEEN

ALARIC

We found a spot to camp in the woods a few hundred yards from the southern road. The border between the Night Court and the day was only a mile away. We'd cross it in the early morning, before the dew dried. If all went according to plan, we'd arrive at the Suriel's palace by late afternoon.

Liana had the fire roaring before Tiernan could place the last log. Turned out the Day Courter was skilled with a bow just as well as he was skilled with a blade. He'd speared two rabbits along the way. One through the eye, and as I cleaned the other, I saw where the arrowhead had punctured its heart. I shook my head, my lips parting.

"When we get back," I said to him, finishing with the skinning, "You need to teach me how to shoot like that."

He smirked from where he sat against a log with Liana between his legs, her head resting against his chest while he stroked her hair. Her eyes were closed, and by the constant drooping and then jolting of her head, I'd say she was doing her best not to fall asleep right there. "If you like," he said. "I thought I could teach Liana, too."

My mood soured at his subtle mention of her training. I didn't want her to fight in this war at all. Every time she trained—got stronger, I had to wonder if It would be enough. Or if I'd lose her in the end, anyway.

If Ricon and his army of Alchemists would slaughter us like they slaughtered my parents at Mt. Ignis. I saw his head cock at the tightening in my jaw, and I turned away, "Yes. She should learn the bow," I said plainly, skewering the rabbit onto sticks Finn sharpened with his dagger.

Finn poked at the fire, adding another log. "Here," he said, holding a hand out for the meat, "I'll do it—you go rest."

I passed him the skewers and set to washing my hands in the creek close to our campsite. There was a lake nearby—if the old map Finn had was to be trusted. There, we could bathe in the morning to save us from arriving covered in dust from the long road and smelling of horse.

Liana would want to change.

Tiernan gestured to a sleeping Liana when I returned to the camp, the aroma of cooking rabbit's meat luring me back.

Take her, he mouthed.

I peeled off my vest and brushed off my tunic, sitting down next to him. Rested my back against the rough bark of the fallen tree. He shifted her into my lap and she stirred, her icy blue eyes flying open for a moment before drifting closed again. I wrapped my arms around her and her weight settled against me. Warm and soft. Somehow, she still smelled good after a day's travel—like soft cotton and tangy marmalade. I breathed in the scent of her, let it calm me.

Tiernan wandered into the woods, likely looking for Arrow—who had caught up to us earlier and then flew off again just after the sun set.

Liana stirred again, and a knife of fear lanced through my chest. Her fear—radiating through my Grace and our bond. She whimpered. I compelled myself to calm and shared the emotion with her. Giving her peace. Her pulse slowed against my chest and her breathing evened out.

I ran my fingers through her wind-tangled hair.

I will protect you. Even from your own dreams.

Her lips parted, and her expression softened into one of utter relaxation.

"That's it," I whispered, holding her closer. "Sleep, my queen."

WE STOPPED for a quick cleaning at the lake. The water was cool, but not cold. The sun was warmer there and would continue to grow warmer the closer we drew to the Day Court. I wondered what magic they used to keep winter's chill from reaching their lands. We passed three sleepy villages, and though we were scrutinized by the Fae dwelling there, none seemed to know who we were—not even Tiernan.

The palace loomed to above us—up a slow-rising hill. It crouched against the earth like a beast made of sand colored stone. The keep was tall in the back with battlements crowning the top and towers on either side. The rest of the palace was walled in and at varying heights, with interconnecting bridges and what looked like a forest growing up through the middle.

Liana gasped as it came into full view, "It's magnificent, isn't it?" she said, her eyes alight with excitement.

"It is," I answered her, "But it's no rival to the palace of night."

She scrunched her eyebrows, considering. Shook her head, "No, but it's a close second."

Liana tried to spur her mare faster, but the rotund creature whinnied and stomped its hooves. "Ugh," she groaned, "This gods-forsaken horse won't go any faster!"

I brushed the dark hair and sweat from my forehead, wishing I'd brought lighter clothes. "Take my horse, if you'd like," I offered her with a challenge in my stare, "But I can't guarantee he won't throw you."

She huffed, rolling her eyes, "Just tell me how to make it go."

I tried not to laugh at her ire and failed, "Squeeze your thighs," I told her, "And then thrust your hips forward in the saddle to give her direction—No, don't pull on the reins like that. That's telling her to stop. Give her her head and then—"

"I haven't taken her head—it's still there isn't it?"

"No, just—" I started, but she did as I told her, and the mare took off down the winding path towards the palace, the sound of my queen's squeals trailing behind it.

Finn and Tiernan trotted up beside me. Tiernan whistled low, and Finn sealed his lips tight against a laugh, clearing his throat.

"Should we..." Finn began, gesturing to where Liana bounced in her saddle as the mare broke into a full run.

"*Alllllaaaaaaaaaaarric,*" she shouted, her voice wobbling with the movements of the horse.

I sighed, giving Finn and Tiernan a wide-eyed stare and a shrug "I suppose we should."

"Bet I can catch her first," Tiernan said, shouting to spur his white mare into a full sprint.

Finn bucked his own steed before giving it its head to follow closely on Tiernan's heels. And for a moment, I pictured it—what life could be like once it was all over. Once there was no more danger, and it was just us—together, helping Liana to rule her court as best as she could until the end of her days. No more worrying about my comrades or my queen. It was a dream worth fighting for. One I would die trying to protect.

CHAPTER SIXTEEN

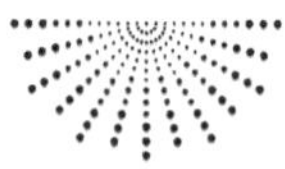

LIANA

Bastards. The damned horse could have killed me! They rode up more concerned about who'd reached me first before they even bothered trying to help slow Scylla. I was still grumpy when we finally reached the main gate of the palace. And it seemed here, the Fae knew who we were despite not wearing our court's colors.

They stopped to gape at us as they milled about the palace. Nobles and servants and courtiers. Not separate but living in harmony—shopping from little market stalls along the walls of the inner ward of the palace.

"Welcome," A red-headed female said, curtsying, a bounce in her step. Her cheeks flecked with tiny spots of brown. "Do you know the way to main palace?"

Alaric pushed ahead of me, blocking the female's line of sight, "Would you be able to show us the way?" he asked, her, standoffish —his voice a brusque timber.

"Of course," I heard her say, "Follow me."

"Alaric," I chastised, trying to kick him from my saddle, moving to get down when I couldn't reach.

"Stay on your horse, Liana," he said—a little too harshly, and I could see how on-edge he was. His eyes wide and watching everything around us. His teeth clamped and grinding together with his nerves.

"Alaric, stop," I said, "Can't you feel it?"

We had reason to be apprehensive, but with the ancient law of Honorem Copulare invoked, it would be an act of war for any of the people of Suriel's court to attack us. But it wasn't the reason I was so calm. With my Grace over emotion, I *felt* the surrounding Fae. There was nothing like hatred radiating off them. They felt honored —maybe a little confused, and a bit apprehensive, but there was no animosity. Only curiosity.

They didn't mean to harm us.

"I do," he sniped, "But that doesn't mean I trust it. Come on, the faster we get to the main palace the better. And where the hell is Edris? He should've been at the gate."

The path wound through the market, past an inner garden and ornate fountain, and through the stables, where we left our horses with a very enthusiastic stable boy.

The main palace was on the far southern side of the inner ward and seemed to grow from the ground itself. A wide stone staircase led to the main entry, and above that were the walkways we could see from the road, connecting the different wings and towers. Through the entrance was a great tree—the largest I'd ever beheld, with white bark and leaves the color of fresh blood.

And as we ascended the staircase, we could see Edris walking around the tree's wide trunk—a female keeping pace with him, a trio of guards flanking them. It was Suriel, I was sure of it. Was Edris *laughing*? Alaric and I shared a look, coming over the top of the stairs.

"Took you long enough," Edris said to Alaric, stepping in to shake my captain's hand. The queen held back with her guards, watching us with a curious glint to her blue-green eyes. "I trust the journey wasn't too taxing."

"It was fine," Alaric said gruffly, and I watched his adam's apple bob as he took in the queen. But she fixed her gaze on Tiernan, who looked away as soon as their eyes met. Then her gaze rested on me, and she stepped forward.

"Welcome to my court," she said in a voice like honey over stone. Her pin-straight long black hair ruffled in the warm breeze, half of it up and the other half down. Suriel's turquoise eyes slanted in consideration, set in a long face of soft features with a full-lipped smile. Beautiful. She looked like a goddess with her exaggerated curves. In her gauzy sunset colored dress and gold neck and arm bands.

I gave her a small nod in lieu of a bow. "Thank you for agreeing to this meeting."

Her gaze flicked to Tiernan again, and I felt his unease seep through my own skin.

"You must all be in need of washing and a good rest," she said, and a petite mouse of a female scurried over from somewhere unseen behind the front walls. "Arin will show you to your chambers, and tonight we'll feast to your arrival."

Seeing the confusion in my expression, Edris turned to Suriel, "As I said before, Your Majesty—there is a very pressing matter to be discussed. My daughter would not have invoked Honorem Copulare if it weren't urgent."

Her eyes hardened, "There will be plenty of time for council on the morrow," she said in a sing-song voice, "This is a momentous occasion. There hasn't been a meeting between the queens of Meloran for an age. Tonight, we celebrate—now please, allow Arin to show you to your chambers. She will get you anything you need."

Edris shrugged, and the queen spun on her heel and walked back the way she came. Her three guardians following closely behind her.

"She dismissed the urgency for council so easily... Edris, you haven't told her why we've come?" I asked him.

He shook his head, "I thought I would leave that to you... and Suriel is a bit standoffish at first, but in the day I've been here she's already softened. She has a good heart—she isn't unlike you."

My brows raised. Queen Suriel had only had her crown for a little over twenty years and was only half a century older than me. I supposed it was possible we held similar, more modern views.

"I'm going with her—she said she'd give me a tour of the palace," Edris said, as though asking for my permission.

Before I could formulate a response, he turned to follow her, "Great! I'll see you at the feast later this evening."

Tiernan stepped up beside me, "I think he's smitten with her."

I cocked my head at my father, seeing the slight bounce in his step, "I think you might be right—though I'm not surprised. I don't think I've ever seen a rival to her beauty."

"I have," Tiernan said, and I turned to find him gazing at my face, a cheeky smirk turning his lips up at one corner.

I shoved him, "Come on, let's go get cleaned up."

"If you'll follow me," Arin said with dimples in her cheeks and a glimmer in her brown eyes, not bothering to check if we were following her when she took off at a near jog around the great tree and into the heart of the palace of Day.

I SUCKED in a breath at the sheer size of the guest quarters when Arin shouldered open the tall, ornately carved door. Finn looked like he approved, with a dumbfounded expression on his usually thoughtful face. Alaric scanned each crevice with calculated precision. And Tiernan strolled into the room as though it belonged to him, pouring a drink of water from a large pitcher set against one wall.

The chamber opened up into a gilded parlour set with plush crème colored sofas stitched with gold embroidery. Transparent red curtains billowed in the gentle breeze pouring in through a wide south-facing window. Beyond, I could see lush forests interspersed with plantations and small farms—and way out into the distance, the ocean gleamed like a polished jewel against the horizon.

"The bedchamber is through there," Arin said, gesturing with a dainty hand to a corridor off to her right, "And there is a dining area through there," she continued, pointing the opposite way with a smile. "The bathing chamber is below the bedchamber—you'll see the staircase in the room."

Only one bedchamber? I opened my mouth to ask her about it, but she was already on her way out, "I'll return to fetch you for the feast this evening. If you should need anything else, there is a bell," she pointed to a brass bell fixed to an iron hanger beside the front entrance, "Just ring and I'll be right up!"

And then she left.

"Fan out," Alaric said the moment the servant had departed. "Search the entire chamber."

Coming back to their senses, my males squared their jaws and did as he commanded them without protest. Tiernan took to the dining area, and Alaric searched the main foyer and parlor, careful to look outside the window as well. Finn made for the bedchamber and I followed him there, admiring the sandstone walls and the generally *warm* feeling of the chamber.

"Is that a..." I trailed off, entering the bedchamber with Finn. The room was enormous—the walls rounded, and the floor covered in plush carpet. But it wasn't the size of the room that caught my attention.

It was the size of the bed. Double the size of mine back at the Night Court—at least. Maybe more. Covered in soft-looking golden sheets, thick pillows of many sizes and several blankets. Gauzy fabric hung from a ring in the ceiling, draping over the entire thing. I wanted to crawl into it and stay there—hide from all the horror of the world.

A childlike joy rushed through me. It reminded me of the forts the seven sisters and I would build when I was a child—though they were smaller, and the netting was more to keep out insects than it was aesthetically pleasing. And Thana would...

I clamped my mouth shut—gritted my teeth to block out the pain in my chest at the mere thought of her.

Alaric and Tiernan entered behind us, and I heard my captain curse at what he saw and turned to find him throwing a fist through his hair. Tiernan didn't look surprised and only sighed.

Finn was the one to break the silence, cocking his head at the enormous bed, "Well, good thing it's big—since there's only one."

CHAPTER SEVENTEEN

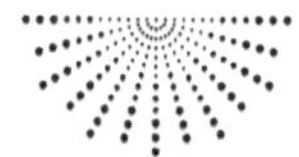

TIERNAN

*E*ntering the feast hall was like walking into a den of wolves. They all stopped in their chatting and drinking to ogle us. Well, to ogle Liana. The queen had sent up a gown for her to wear—crusted in a thousand sparkling blue gems, cut low in the front and tight around her waist. It had been near impossible not to want to tear it from her body the moment I'd seen her in it. The queen had even had servants come to our chamber and do Liana's hair, piling it atop her head in a beautiful crown of silver locks.

I knew Suriel, and she was a wise and fair ruler. But it seemed odd how she was acting. Was she trying to impress Liana? Or trying to befriend her? Or was something more sinister in fact going on as Alaric thought.

Even though she never voiced it in front of me, I always thought she would be open to having a relation with the Night Court. It wasn't like her to uphold the antiquated views of others. No, there was nothing sinister about it. Suriel was hoping to win Liana's trust —to build a lasting impression of her people. The prospect of open trade between nations could have an incredible impact for her people, who were rich in wine and rice, but poor in grain and cattle.

The large oval table was occupied by Queen Suriel, wearing a russet orange gown—her crown perched atop her hair like a yellow canary, and Edris, who sat to her right, and several esteemed nobles.

I stiffened when my gaze fell upon him—a sneering expression twisting his face and darkening his pale features. My uncle sat on the other side of Edris, languidly chewing a piece of roast pork while he stared at me.

"What is it," Liana whispered, leaning in to my side and brushing her fingers lightly across the back of my hand.

I shivered. "It's nothing," I said, pulling her arm through mine.

"Come!" said the queen, rising from her seat, her cheeks stained red from too much drink, "Please, sit down—sit down!"

I gave Liana's hand a reassuring squeeze and led her to the table. Alaric and Finn moved to sit where the servants indicated a couple seats down from where the queen sat—leaving Liana to sit to the left of the Queen of Day and across from her father, and I to sit next to her, and across from my uncle.

My stomach turned violently at the nearness. I had left his estate years ago but seeing him there put me right back in that younger self's skin. Cowering from the whip of his belt as it bit into flesh that was already raw. Begging to be heard over the deafening silence within his walls.

Liana's fingers dug into my thigh under the table, her fingers tipped with searing heat. I turned and found her eyes aglow in a mix of gold and red—her gaze fixed on my uncle. Of course...

Idiot.

She could feel my emotions—and thanks to the bond, gods knew what she saw in my mind. I laid my hand over hers, tugged it until she looked at me. "It isn't worth it," I told her in a low voice, grateful for the cover of Edris and Suriel's laughter.

She took a moment, but I watched her begin to calm. Then she turned back to her food, her expression grim.

He should pay for what he did to you.

I jolted. My spine tingling when her voice rang out inside my skull, half choking on my swallow of wine.

Finding the tether between us, I spoke down the length of it, as calmly as I could. *And he will. In time.*

"I trust you're *enjoying* your new home?" My uncle asked, his mouth still full of half-chewed meat.

Overhearing my uncle's comment, Suriel leaned in to give me a forlorn look across the table, "Ah yes, my Tiernan—well, I suppose not anymore. I was sad to see you go," she sighed, holding out her glass to be refilled with wine, "But I can see now why you didn't return." Her gaze cut to Liana, whose hand froze under mine.

Liana bit her bottom lip, swallowing the blush in her cheeks.

Alaric cleared his throat, "Tiernan has been a valuable member of Liana's guard. I thank you for releasing him to us."

"Hmmmmm," she replied while swallowing down more drink. "I hope you feel welcome back at court and that you'll return whenever you like... I do miss your company," she finished with a sultry tone to her voice. A thread of heat seared down my spine and it took every ounce of my self-control not to shake my head at her.

Her appetite for pleasure was always ravenous—but it was worse when she drank. And she wasn't superb at taking *no* for an answer.

A snort from behind her and I saw Salar's look of distaste. As the captain of her guard and the one who chose me, I couldn't blame him for being upset at my choice. The other two guards I never got to know well.

Even though it'd been months, she still hadn't replaced me.

Edris resumed polite conversation with Suriel, tearing her attentions away from me. Thank the gods.

Liana did not hide her discomfort and took a long swallow of her own drink, her eyes widening at the taste.

I nudged her shoulder, "Quite good, isn't it?"

She smiled, but it didn't reach her eyes.

It was plain to see she was restless. War waited on our doorstep back home, and here we were breaking bread with her supposed enemy. I wanted to ease the tension in her shoulders and smooth the crease in her forehead. Kiss away the frown from her lips.

Liana drained another glass of wine—picking at the foreign meal of salted pork and charred fruit. Lost in her own thoughts.

"It doesn't taste like it," I said, staying her hand before she could take another swallow of the summer wine, "But it's a strong blend. I would sip it slowly."

CHAPTER EIGHTEEN

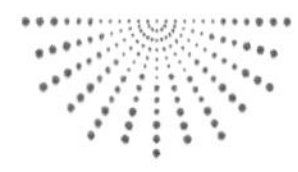

LIANA

I should've listened to Tiernan.

By the time the nobles at the other end of the table were making ready to leave, the room swayed before my eyes. The edges of my vision were hazy as if I was seeing through a thin sheet of fog.

I'd had enough of listening to Tiernan's ass of an uncle make passive aggressive small talk to his nephew, who I could feel getting more and more riled and upset with each word out of the old fool's thin lips.

And I was *done* wearing the ridiculous gown Suriel had stuffed me into.

The jewels crusting the hem and the sleeves were heavy and scratched against my skin every time I moved. The corset was too tight, and the servant pulled my hair back so severely I was afraid it would give up trying to hold its shape and spring from my skull.

Ugh. Though I'd slept alright curled against Alaric in the woods the night before—his warm leather and vanilla scent and his Grace enveloping me in calm—I was utterly spent and more than ready to be done with forced pleasantries. The faster I slept, the faster I could wake and do what I came here to do and get back to my own palace.

More than that, I was beginning to worry about Kade and would have to reach through the bond tomorrow to check on him. I thought I'd have heard something from him by now...

Alaric spoke with a male to his left, conversing about the differences in our courts, and the ways in which they were the same. Finn conversed animatedly with the Queen, shouting to be heard over the distance between them. Him, Edris, and Suriel laughing as they all drank their fill of wine.

Tiernan hadn't had more than a glass. Alaric even less so, and I was glad at least two of us maintained our sobriety. The room tilted again, and I felt the roiling mixture of fire and ice in my core spinning in confusion at the queasiness.

I shouldn't be here.

As if sensing my need to leave, Tiernan brushed my arm, and I leaned back to look at him, my body swaying more than it should've.

"Can I take you back to our chambers?"

I didn't trust myself to speak aloud, so I threw a resounding *yes* to him through our bond.

"I thought so," he said, and sneakily helped me to stand. I squared my shoulders and attempted to stand tall—blinking the strange film from my eyes.

Clearing my throat, and bracing my weight against Tiernan, I said to the queen, "Thank you for the meal. I look forward to meeting with you first thing in the morning."

Her grin grew, and she squinted at me through the haze of her own drink, "Oh, won't you stay?" she asked, "I was about to call for some music?"

Gods. The idea of dancing nearly made me throw up what little of the spicy food I'd choked down. "I—" I began, but Tiernan interjected, sensing my discomfort.

"The Queen needs her rest, Your Majesty. Our journey was long."

Her smile faltered, but she didn't argue any further. Righting the crown atop her head with an undignified pout, "As you wish."

Alaric moved to stand, cutting off mid-conversation with the male sitting next to him.

"Stay," I implored him. "I'm just going to bed. Please—finish your meal."

My captain shared a long look with Tiernan, and his unease pawed at me with insistent strokes. "Fine," Alaric finally said, "We'll finish up here and be right behind you."

Are you alright? He added through the bond.

I nodded. *Fine. A little too much wine...*

His brows rose, and he pressed his lips into a thin line to avoid laughing.

I rolled my eyes. *Do me a favor?*

Anything.

Make that male's, I thought, glancing at Tiernan's sour-faced uncle, *night as awful as you possibly can.*

His head cocked to one side.

Trust me, I practically shouted down the bond, *he deserves it.*

"Let's go," I whispered to Tiernan, and he took me by the arm, bracing my weight with his and led me from the dining chamber.

"GET me out of this godsforsaken thing," I whined, fumbling with the laces at my back.

"Here," Tiernan said, finishing his sweep of the bedchamber, "Stop it, you'll never be able to untie that yourself."

He gently swatted my hands away, and I braced myself on the bedpost, wondering why the room smelled of jasmine and hot cedar. The mixture was heady and erotic, alternately calming and exciting my senses.

"She sent servants to put me in the damned thing—she should have sent them back to get me out of it. *Gods,* these jewels weigh more than I do!"

Tiernan chuckled, unweaving the corset up my back with slow, practiced precision. With each deepening breath I could take as it loosened, I became more and more lightheaded. Using the bedpost as more of a crutch than a brace.

"There," he said, tugging the gown down to pool in a mass of gossamer, silk and jewels at my feet. "Better?"

I swayed trying to step out of the tangle of fabric, nearly fell. Tiernan caught me with a strong arm hooked around my middle. I blinked my eyes back into focus. "What was in that wine? Did she poison me?"

His hair fell into his face when he shook his head, "No—she didn't poison you. I *did* warn you the wine was strong," he said pointedly, righting me back on my feet. "Sit down, let help you get into bed."

"Did I make a fool of myself?" I asked, sitting down hard on the edge of the mattress—sighing when I sunk deep into it's soft embrace.

"Don't be ridiculous. You were perfectly regal," he said with a wink, "If anyone should be embarrassed, it's Suriel."

Tiernan helped me out of my shoes—pulled the stockings from my legs, letting his fingertips trail over my skin. Gooseflesh rose in their wake and I shivered. Then I remembered something she'd said to him and my chest tightened.

"Did you and The Day Queen ever… I mean did you—"

"Lie with her?"

Unable to meet his stare, I laid back onto the bed, staring up at the wisp-thin netting tapering up to the ceiling. "Did you?"

He set my leg back down on the bed and leaned over me, putting his face parallel to mine.

"No," he said, and I knew he told the truth. He smirked, "But that's not to say she didn't want to."

Ugh. I shoved him off me and he fell onto the bed with a disgruntled *ooomff.*

"Who wouldn't want to—have you seen yourself? The depictions of the gods hardly compare."

The canopy spun again, and I groaned, covering my eyes. But that only seemed to make it worse.

"You should sleep," Tiernan said and lifted my head onto a pillow. He leaned down and the warmth of him pressed against me. He laid a kiss on my forehead and my heart sputtered. The tether between us gave a small tug.

I grabbed him by his tunic when he made to pull away, and his shoulders pulled inwards. Opening myself up to *feel* him, I found that he radiated pain.

My jaw clenched, and my stomach roiled at the ugliness. It was his uncle—having to endure his company had shaken Tiernan, and I understood why. I'd seen what his uncle did to him. Giving no sympathy for his parent's death. Ignoring him. Only paying him any mind if it was to punish him with the whip of his belt or the sting of his knuckles across Tiernan's jaw.

He would pay for his sins—whether in this life, or the next.

"Don't pay him another thought," I said, and Tiernan looked away. I pulled his face back to me and pressed my lips softly against his. His hand tightened around mine and the dark emotions abated —just a little.

"Goodnight," he said as I pulled away, falling back onto the silky-soft sheets.

I rubbed the back of his hand. Gave him a reassuring smile. "Goodnight, Tiernan."

CHAPTER NINETEEN

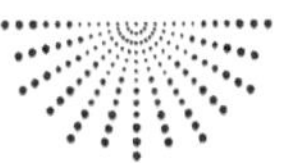

KADE

The darkness scattered like smoke in the wind—blowing away as I retook my Fae form to reveal a corridor of the palace. I rushed down the marble tile in long, fast strides, my body readjusting to the weight of bone and muscle. Travel by smoke was convenient, but it always left me feeling weak, heavy, and with the acrid taste of ashes on my tongue.

I leaned out the nearest window and spat out the foul black ichor before hurrying on to the council chambers. They wouldn't have summoned me at this hour if it wasn't important.

It wasn't difficult to find the tether of the Immortal Bond. Since Liana left there'd been a hollowness in my chest. As if every mile she put between herself and I, the thinner the tether stretched and the more the absence of her burrowed into me. I latched onto the link between us and hurtled my thoughts through it. *I know it's late,* I said, *but the council has called me—I think the envoy has returned to the palace.*

Doing as Finn explained before he left, I forced what I was seeing to travel through the bond, too.

There came no response. I worked harder to maintain the connection, hoping she could see what I saw. Hear my calls.

I shoved the doors open, turning so my wings wouldn't catch on the frame. Four sets of eyes found mine. Only half the council members had come at the summons. They stood around one end of the long table, their faces pale and drawn. A putrid odor permeated the council chamber. I recoiled from it as if it were a physical blow, my eyes watering and nostrils flared.

"What is it?" I demanded, searching for the answer in their close-lipped frowns. "And what in the name of the gods is that smell?"

"The envoy has returned," the court's baron of finance answered me, looking nauseated. He gaged, cringing.

The room held no others. And I had seen no riders when I swept the northern roads this morning. "Well, where are they? What have they said?"

"They've said nothing," the rotund one with the beard snarled, stepping away from the table to reveal a wooden chest standing open on the table.

My stomach dropped. I stepped in closer to the table and the three males parted, allowing me to pass. I knew what I would find, and yet I *had* to look. To be certain.

I peered over the top of the chest. A finger of fire raced up my spine. My stomach curdled like soured milk.

It was grotesque. It was the envoy—that much was certain. It was easy enough to tell by the severed hand still baring the ring seal of the Night Court. But there were four hands. Four eyes. Four tongues. Stitched together into the disturbed shape of a monstrous creature with a gaping maw—the flesh paled and putrid. The base of the chest coated in a thick layer of crimson grime.

Swallowing the urge to vomit, I stepped away from it.

"We must send word to the queen. She *must* return."

I wasn't sure who'd said it. Didn't care.

If I succeeded in allowing her to see through my eyes, she already knew. The envoy had returned... in pieces.

"I will," I responded. "I'll need to tell Silas, too." I stalked from the council chamber, letting the fire build and writhe in my core.

They called after me, asking me when I'd be leaving—how long it would take for Liana to return. Asking me all sorts of questions I stopped hearing.

Vaulting from the terrace at the end of the corridor, I flew north toward Silas and the Horde—hoping I could make it to the border by dawn.

The message was clear. Ricon had no intention of talking terms or coming to any sort of compromise that would lessen the bloodshed. He meant to wipe out any who would stand in his way of getting Liana's crown. There would be no mercy. It was time to prepare for war.

CHAPTER TWENTY

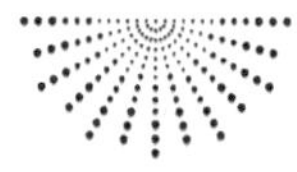

LIANA

I gagged, heaving in a long shuddering breath.

Eyes wide in the dark, I bolted upright in the bed. Arms reached out for me—tried to grab me, and I yelped, backing away. My pulse a drum-beat echo in my ears. I backed up into a wall of solid, naked muscle. I lashed out, trying to find my attacker, but my eyes wouldn't adjust.

Strong hands bound my wrists in their vise-like grip and I thrashed, trying to get free.

"Liana!" My name was a command—loud and insistent. "Liana, it's us. You're safe."

The wall of muscle behind me reached out to rub my back, and I flinched, my spine going rigid at first before my breathing and pulse calmed, evening out.

I found the curve of Alaric's face in the trickle of moonlight and reached out for him, collapsing into his arms.

"Was it a bad dream?" Finn asked from somewhere to my right while Tiernan moved in closer to continue rubbing my back.

I shook my head against Alaric's tunic, "No, it was a vision. From Kade."

Alaric stiffened beneath me, his breath hitching. And Tiernan's hand stilled, dropping from my back. "What did you see?" he asked.

My stomach roiled, the acid rising into my throat at the memory. It wasn't so much the sight—though it was morbidly grotesque—no, it was the *smell*. That awful, putrid rank of decaying flesh and the strong metallic tang of clotted blood. I swallowed, hauling in clean, crisp air through my nose to clear it.

"The envoy returned," I told them, "The Mad King sent them back in pieces."

They were all silent after that and I wished someone would say something. *Anything.* But they didn't, not for long, arduous minutes.

"Come," Finn said, "I'll help you dress," and rose from the bed to light a lantern.

"I'll call for some tea," Tiernan added, padding to the front door to give the bell two sharp rings.

Alaric took me by the arms and held me back to look into my eyes, "Queen Suriel will see reason. She'll help us," he said with a forced smile.

I wanted to believe him, but I wasn't sure he believed it himself.

"Your Majesty," I said, bowing at the waist in greeting. The sun had only just risen, and there was still a shroud of morning mist clinging to the earth. Making the hot air seem thick and hazy. "Thank you for meeting with me so early."

The council chamber in the palace of day looked more like a drawing room. There was a table in the middle, but big-puffy armchairs and wide fat cushions sat against the walls as though for her council members to relax or meditate. The whole room had a warm feel, clothed in golds, reds, and burnt orange fabrics and finery, bathed in the growing dawn light.

It was very... informal.

"Yes," said Suriel, pinching the bridge of her nose, dark circles under her eyes marred her otherwise flawless features. I mentally thanked Tiernan for his wisdom in calling for the ginger root tea to soothe the aftereffects of my over drinking…

"I'm told the reason you've requested the old law of Honorem Copulare is urgent, but I'm sure it could've waited until a more agreeable hour."

I shook my head, "No, it couldn't wait any longer."

Her brows raised, but she nodded, "I apologize—please do unburden yourself, you look as though ready to burst with it…"

My hand shook at my side and my heart sputtered in my chest. *She will help us.* She must.

I filled my lungs with a steadying breath—no sense in easing into it… "King Ricon II has returned—he didn't fall in the battle of Mt. Noctis."

Her face screwed up into a confused scowl. She allowed the information to marinate between us, not uttering a word.

After a beat or two of silence, I continued, "He and his army camp in the northern reaches of the Wastes."

"His army?"

A flood of ice rushed into my gut, "Ten thousand strong. Alchemists, Fae, and Draconians."

"Alchemists working alongside Fae?"

I'd just told her an army of ten thousand waits on my doorstep, and *that* is the bit she picked out.

I didn't oblige her with an answer.

"We've come to ask for your help," I said, and her teal eyes flicked up to meet mine, gleaming with something like fear, "Our Horde army numbers close to five thousand—it won't be enough to defeat him."

She cocked her head at me, squinting her eyes, "Why? Why has he returned/ What does he want?"

"Isn't it obvious?" I asked her, clasping my hands to keep them from trembling, forcing my voice to remain strong and true, "He wants what was taken from him—his crown."

"*Your* crown?"

I could tell she was weighing her options. Her asking me if it was *my* crown he meant to take told me she was already shying away from the idea of helping us. "Yes," I answered, "But once he's wiped out the Fae of my court and claimed his prize, what's stopping him from wanting to *expand* his empire?"

She snarled, pacing the pretty carpet in her bare feet—her shoulders tensed and shaking, "You don't know that!" she nearly shouted, "You don't know that he'll come here. It was his daughter who stole his crown—it wasn't us. It wasn't the Day Court!"

I put my hands out in a calming gesture, "That may be true, but it was *your* court that came to aid us in the battle at Mt. Noctis. His followers died by Day Court hands, too."

"And you think he'll want retribution? Blood for blood?"

"I don't know, Suriel. All I know is that together, we stand a chance of defeating him. But neither of us can alone."

She paced her way to the only window in the room, leaning out of it and gulping down air as if the council chamber itself was suffocating her.

"I know this is a lot—" I began, but my vision wavered, blurring, and a forceful tug at my chest had me crying out. I winced, falling to my knees on the carpet.

Suriel spun, "Liana..."

But her words and everything else around me vanished.

I shivered, the cold pricking at my bare arms. Opening my eyes —no, not my eyes, *Kade's* eyes, I found myself high above the ground, hovering in midair.

They're coming, Kade spoke in my mind and I looked north, the blood turning to ice in my veins. My heart stopping. It couldn't be...

Far into the distance, an army marched over the frost-covered earth. From the air they looked like ants—thousand upon *thousands* of ants. Marching south.

The clatter of their shields and armor and their booted feet pounding dirt a symphony of dread. Rippling through the air and into my soul.

An arrow ripped through the sky, its obsidian tip glinting in the sunlight as it headed straight for Kade. He dropped just in time for it to soar over him.

Get out of there! I screamed inside his head and he spun away, casting me from his mind. I tumbled back down the tether, coming back to myself in Suriel's council chambers, my fingers digging into the floor like claws.

"Liana," Alaric said, and I found his wide steel-blue eyes when I lifted my heavy head. "What is it? Was it Kade? What happened?"

They were supposed to wait outside, but taking a cursory look around, I could see all of Queen Suriels's guards and mine were now crowding the council chamber.

I needed an answer. *Now.* It was time to leave.

Alaric helped me stand, and I turned back to the Queen of Day, who looked at me incredulously, "You bound yourself to one of your royal guards?" she asked, her hand fluttering at her chest, shock plain in her features.

"No," I answered her, "I bound myself to *all* of them."

She opened her mouth to say something, but I silenced her with a glare and a raised hand, "The Mad King's army marches south. They'll be at the borders of my court in a fortnight—maybe less. I *need* to know if I have your support." I released my hold on Alaric, standing on my own, resolute. My jaw squared, "Will you help us?"

Her royal guards exchanged animated whispers, their brows furrowed and faces grim.

"Quiet," she barked at them, walking with slow, measured steps to the table. Setting her palms against the smooth wood. She panted, her eyes wild and searching.

Edris moved into the room from where he stood near the door, "Your Majesty, if I may—"

"I need a moment!"

"We don't have a moment to waste."

She hung her head and sealed her eyes. Her shoulders tensed. When she turned, it was Edris she spoke to, an apology in her eyes, "This is not our war," she said. "And there's no reason for me to believe Ricon means me or my court any harm."

Frost covered my fingertips, climbing like vines up my arms. "Suriel, if you don't help us, you're condemning us to death."

Her eyes gleamed and her chin quivered, "I'm so sorry," she said, "But I cannot ask my people to fight—to *die* for... I'm sorry, I just can't." Queen Suriel rushed past me and out the door to the council chamber. I watched her go, her head bent, her guards following at her heels.

Edris reached out to stop her, but she brushed him off, "Your Majesty, wait," he said, turning back to me, "You go. The Night Court needs you," he said, "I'll stay here. I'll speak to her. She will see reason—she must."

"Stay if you like," I said, my voice sounding oddly detached, "But she's made up her mind. We are alone in this war."

My fathers' gaze hardened, and his lips pressed tightly together. Edris narrowed his sights on Alaric, "Keep my daughter safe," he said through gritted teeth, "I'll return to court as soon as I can."

CHAPTER TWENTY-ONE

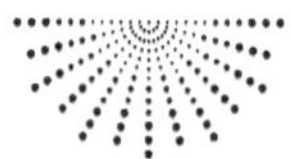

FINN

I didn't have to be Graced with power over emotion to notice the change in the mood of our party on the journey home. We hardly spoke. Liana was the quietest of all of us. She rode ahead, alone, maintaining a steady pace.

How she must feel.... as if she'd failed her court. I wish I could tell her she hadn't and that the Day Court's armies wouldn't have made a difference, but we both knew that wasn't true.

I racked my brain for a solution but could find nothing plausible. The Mad King was coming, and with or without the Day Court army, we would have to be ready when they did. But those were problems for tomorrow.

As we neared the palace, the sun dipped below the horizon and the full moon shone brighter, marking the death of another day.

The ivory castle milled with Fae eager to return home for the evening, and those who passed us on their travels south bowed to their queen or welcomed her home, but it was as if she couldn't see them, blinded by her own grief. Her hand tight on the reins, wincing with each step of her horse.

The ride had taken its toll on her, and I wondered why she didn't heal the aches that so obviously were causing her discomfort.

Alaric rode beside me, his head bent, and brows furrowed. His warm breath clouding in the frigid air.

The telltale sound of wings slicing wind had me whipping my head upwards, finding Kade as he descended from one of the terraces to meet us. Liana had already told him the Day Queen's answer through the bond, and she said his response was so vulgar she dared not repeat it to us. I could only image the amount of profanities he'd spewed aloud, never mind what Liana heard in his thoughts.

He hadn't told the council yet. Alaric would do that tonight, and Kade would retrieve Silas from the front lines so Liana could meet with him and the rest of the council in the morning to discuss what needed to be done to prepare.

What *could* be done.

Kade came to an easy landing next to Liana's mare, taking the reins to stop the animal in its slow walk. I saw her shoulders shaking and my insides knotted—my chest collapsing at the sight of her broken and defeated. He pulled her from the mare and into his arms where she shook against him, convulsing with the strength of her sobs.

"Get her out of here," I heard Alaric gently order Kade as we neared. My brother nodded to his captain with a hard, pained expression and scooped Liana into his arms, flying her the rest of the way to the palace, leaving her mare to make its own way back to the stables.

We—Alaric, Tiernan, and I—hadn't seen what they saw. No one else had. A finger of ice pressed into my gut.

"I'll need you on watch tonight," Alaric said, not lifting his head when I pulled up alongside him. "Tiernan will relieve you in the early morning."

"Alright."

"And Finn," he said, looking up, "She needs you."

I didn't catch his meaning.

"Give her one night of peace before the start of it all tomorrow. A formal announcement will need to be made to the court.

And then…"

He didn't need to finish. I understood the weight of what he implied. And then we would make ready for the battle to come. We'd do everything within our power to lessen the amount of bloodshed. And to protect her. Until the end.

I nodded gravely, spurring my horse into a gallop, eager to get him stabled and up to Liana's chambers.

THE FARAWAY EXPRESSION hadn't left her face. She stared into the hearth in the parlor as though it held the answers to her many questions.

Kade had left moments ago after he promised a swift return. She'd squeezed his hand, but said nothing, taking another small sip of icy water when he moved away, sighing as he flew from the terrace.

I knelt in front of her, "Come with me," I asked her, holding out a hand. Her gaze drifted towards me, looking to my hand, trying to read my expression.

The muscles in her jaw twitched, but she set down her glass and pressed her frost-covered fingers into my palm. I stood, lifting her from the armchair and she followed without question or complaint from the parlor, down the corridor, and into the bedchamber.

She dropped my hand as we approached the bed, and my pulse quickened. "Take off your dress."

Her vacant expression morphed into one of confusion, "Why?"

"Trust me."

She swallowed, and undid the fastening above her breasts, letting the thick cloak she wore fall to the floor. I helped her with the corset strings and her dress and trousers fell too.

My heart leap into my throat at the sight of her, bare, her nipples standing at attention against the chill breeze. Her stomach muscles tight and her shoulders tense.

"Lie on your stomach."

She pursed her lips, but did as I asked, crawling onto the bed and laying stiffly against the feather-filled coverlet. My cock hardened in my trousers, and I bit the inside of my cheek to keep myself on task. The ice that had collected in my bones vanished. This wasn't about me, or what I wanted. It was about her.

I extinguished the lantern next to her bed and pulled the bar of hardened oils from my vest, unwrapping it from the silk cloth and crawled onto the bed next to her.

"Finn…?"

I hushed her, moving so my knees rested on either side of her hips. "Try to relax," I said, coating my hands with the oil. The scents of lavender and honeysuckle filled the room, and her muscles uncoiled beneath me.

She sighed as I worked the oil into her back, pressing and kneading and rubbing out the knots under her skin. Within a few moments, the tension in her buttocks and neck all but vanished, and her breathing evened out. After an hour more she had all but become one with the bed.

The knots were still there, but not as pronounced, and her pulse had slowed back into its normal rhythm. Her skin was still cool to the touch, but not near frozen as it was before. I couldn't tell if she was still awake.

I leaned in and laid a kiss against the back of her neck, breathing in her sweet earthy scent mixed with the heady aroma of the oil still clinging to her. She shivered, and the motion reverberated down her body, awakening my senses.

She turned beneath me, flipping over so we were face to face. Her eyes were sultry and sleepy, and her hair was a mess, bunched up atop her head like a bird's nest. I couldn't help the smile twitching at the corner of my mouth.

"How do you feel?" I asked her.

"Better," she whispered, trailing a finger up the length of my torso, setting my nerve-endings ablaze. Her path stopped where the thin cloth of the tunic met the dip in my throat and it looked as though something had occurred to her because she licked her lips and swallowed, and her heartbeat quickened.

The smell of her desire flooded my senses all at once and her eyes lit like sapphires in the dark. "Make love to me," she said.

As if she already sensed my answer—and she probably had—her hand curled into my tunic and pulled me down, pressing her lips to mine. I deepened the kiss, sensing just how close to the edge she was. She walked the thin line between her desire to have me—to escape reality, and to give in to the torment I aimed to wash from her mind.

I pressed my hand to her chest, my fingers curling around her ribcage. Her skin incredibly soft against my calloused palm. The other I curled deep into the satiny strands of her hair, drawing her closer still—thinking there was no measure of closeness that would ever be enough. I'd hold her with me always. Keep her safe and warm and smiling for as long as I could.

CHAPTER TWENTY-TWO

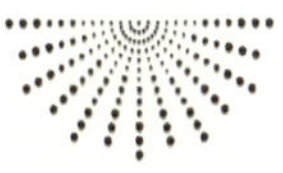

LIANA

He touched me like I was the most precious thing in the world. A rare and fragile gem he was honored to hold. His hands were firm, but gentle where they squeezed and kneaded in my hair and on my skin. I reached down to unfasten his trousers, and he lifted his head. The sight of his dark hair, his eyes glinting in the sliver of moonlight lighting my bedchamber had an ache spreading deep in my belly and between my legs.

The moment I unhooked the final button, he yanked them down to his ankles and kicked them free. His cock pulsed, and his eyes lit with glowing desire. But he made no move to enter me, settling down slowly and purposefully between my thighs.

It coaxed the fire I'd missed the past couple of days back to life, flickering within my core, sending warmth to my extremities.

Finn's gaze roved over me, admiring and appreciating every inch of my flesh. His breathing quickened, and his wings grew taught with anticipation. I reached a tentative hand up, running a finger down the inside of the web-like limb. He gasped, his eyes closing against the sensation.

"*Gods*, Liana…"

"Does it feel good?"

He gritted his teeth, "You have no idea."

"What about this," I asked, reaching down between my legs to take hold of his cock in my hand, rubbing it at the same time as I caressed his wing. He spasmed at the dual sensation, almost convulsing as I wound the bead of wetness at the tip of his length around the whole head, stroking the spot just below the tip.

My own wetness grew, dampening my thighs. It *ached* to be sated.

He groaned, and my back arched as his cock brushed my opening. He jerked at the contact, his eyes opening to reveal a blaze of gold searing down into me. Finn.

My Finn.

My core tightened at the exquisite span of his wings as they caught the moonlight, the expanse of his broad shoulders tapering down to the slender, defined *thrust* of his hips as my hand fell away and he penetrated me. All the breath ran from my lungs at the satiating pressure of him inside me, awakening my senses, setting my mind on fire—erasing every dark, numbing thought and replacing them with only one. Him.

I cried out, and he eased back, his body tensing. I tore the tunic from his torso with clawed hands, needing to see him—all of him. Feel the power of the muscle flexing under the surface of his skin with each deliberate movement of our bodies as they worked in tandem. My hips moving of their own accord, deepening his steady movements.

The quickening came hard and swift, building to a precipice, leaving me staring down in wonder at the steep drop, aching to fall over it and tumble headlong down, down, until there wasn't a sane thought left in my mind.

He kissed me again, and it was frantic, the press of his lips hard as he pushed into me, climbing his own cliff. On the cusp of his own release. He moaned against my lips and I melted at the rawness of the feelings crashing through me, over me, like a tide dragging me out to sea—only I didn't fight against it, I reached for it, begging it, take me, *take me!*

Our bodies tightened against each other, locking together like a door in a frame, and we came together, falling over the edge in a tumultuous roar of hot breaths, howling moans, and fingertips burrowed into unyielding muscle.

CHAPTER TWENTY-THREE

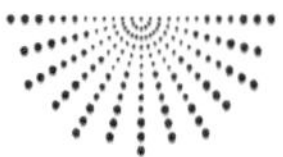

LIANA

The Horde camp wreaked of molten metal, unwashed bodies, and campfire smoke. It wrinkled my nose and gave the whole place the miasmal atmosphere of a hawk staring down a mouse. Almost, but not quite ready to strike.

But anywhere was better than being at the palace. Curled inward at the crushing weight on my shoulders—that weight compounded by the sidelong stares of anyone I passed in the bustling corridors. I'd done my duty and addressed my court, standing in front of each and every noble who could attend the assembly within a day's notice.

The gathering of fifty Fae felt like a crowd of hundreds.

The reaction of my people ranged from shock, to disbelief, to outrage spoken in harsh whispers or shouted outright for all to hear. But the numbness still clung to my bones, so I only spoke my piece and then left—their shouts fading the further I moved away from the assembly hall.

Everyone would know by now. Word had likely spread to even the smallest of villages, like the one the Horde army now camped in. But they had evacuated this one almost a week prior. The people who once inhabited it gone to stay with family or in Inns and cottages paid for by the crown. And by the look of this village, one of the last on route north to the border—wherever they went, it was likely an improvement.

Small, ramshackle huts and buildings formed two parallel lines down the middle, with a forge at one end, and a mill at the other. And sequestered atop a small sloping hill to the south, the noble lord of the area's manor house stood erect, with a sturdy stone exterior, a high piqued roof and a wide double chimney puffing out clouds of soot and smoke.

I didn't have to know him to know he did not deserve his post. Leaving his entrusted area to rot and wither while he lived in ignorant bliss on his hilltop. Pathetic.

"You're awake," Alaric said, turning from where he sat at a rough wooden desk. "I'll call for something to eat." Without another word, he rose and slipped out through the slit in the fabric of our tent. He'd been quiet the last week since we returned to the palace. Though I wasn't much better. I found the only way to beat the wretched despair dragging me down was to throw myself into my training.

I trained day in and day out and had the marks to prove it. Tiernan trained me in sword and bow. Kade trained me in fire and strength. And Finn taught me how to anticipate attacks before they happened, and to find the weak points in my opponents.

And perhaps most importantly, Alaric and I trained together, blocking each other's influence. If we were ever face to face with the Mad King again—we'd need to be prepared.

I was getting better. Stronger. And faster. But would it be enough?

They slept soundly, Kade snoring softly, splayed out on his back atop a bed fit for a toddler—his arms and legs hanging from the edges onto the dirt floor. Finn slept next to me in the fur-covered bed, his knees still curled up from where they rested behind mine only a few moments before. Tiernan's bed was empty. Gods knew where he'd gone…

But of course, in his absence Arrow rested on a coatrack, his head tucked in as though sleeping, but I could see his little beady eyes watching me even in the dim light.

I climbed from the bed as quietly and with as little movement as I could manage, trying not to wake Finn. But the second my feet hit the floor, the vibrations coiled up through the soles of my feet. The *thump, thump, thump,* of hundreds of feet marching—shaking the ground.

And then I heard them. The clamor of metal. The whooshing of wind through bodies pressed tightly together. And the audible clomping of boots over hard-packed dirt.

Silas had been sending our forces in waves to the border, a few hundred at a time. They arrived at the encampment from the main Horde fort to the south, armored and bearing precious supplies before they were sent off to the front—leaving room for the next group to take rest before the next long march.

Kade and Finn stirred in their sleep, their eyes fluttering open to the raucous noise.

"It's just the next group leaving camp," I whispered to them, "Go back to sleep, it'll pass soon."

Kade buried his head under a pillow, and Finn rolled over on his other side. The flight here had tired them the night before, burdened by the weight of Tiernan, Alaric, and I. Their eyes were already half-closed before they could even make it to their beds.

"That's it," I said, slipping away, "Go back to sleep."

Hurriedly, I dressed in my new trousers—they were light, yet warmer than the thickest wool. Darius had insisted that if my mind was set on wearing trousers, I'd at least be seen wearing ones that fit me properly instead of the hand-me-downs I'd brought from the Isle of Mist.

Tugging on my boots and a long jacket, I slipped outside into the cold light of day—my eyes rebelling against the sudden onslaught of gray tinged light.

I squinted at the mass of bodies diligently marching their way out from the town, heading north. As my eyes adjusted, I realized none noticed me. And really, I didn't think they noticed much of anything at all. Moving closer, I found grim faces shadowed under the heavy steel of their helms. Heads bent. Pale skinned.

They marched as if to certain death. My stomach dropped at the sight. A tendril of ice chasing a shiver up my spine. They looked like dead men—empty corpses propelled forward by nothing more than their sense of duty and the smallest sliver of hope that perhaps their lives wouldn't be wasted.

I could see it—but more than that I could *sense* it. My Grace of emotion opened up of its own accord, swallowing up their despair and their fear and their dread and their regrets. Their emotions roiled within me, making me gag against the vulgar, unfiltered truth of it.

Not even one of them thought we could win this… And thinking like that…

We've already lost.

I threw up the mental wall around my mind like Alaric taught me, blocking out all the pain and misery. Sealing up the cracks. A glint of shining steel caught my eye, and I turned to find Silas standing off to the side of the road where the legion of his army marched—seeing them off, ensuring they maintained formation.

Unclenching my fists, I ran over to him, my boots slipping on the half-frozen earth. "Silas," I breathed, and he turned to zero in on me, wide-eyed.

"Liana? What in the gods—"

I shook my head. "Stop them," I said, gesturing wildly to the hundreds of male and female warriors still steadily moving as one unit.

"What for?"

"Just do it, Silas."

He pursed his lips and a glint of condescending annoyance crossed his bright eyes, but after a moment he gave in. Shrugged and heaved a rasping sigh.

Placing his fingers between his lips, he blew the loudest, longest whistle I'd ever had the misfortune to hear. "Halt!" he bellowed and as one the unit braked, turning to face their captain before pressing their feet firmly to the earth, squared towards us.

They looked at us but did not see us. Their eyes glazed. My heart broke for them. Once they noticed who I was, they knelt. Falling in groups to one knee, like a wave of dominos blown over by a rogue wind.

But this was *not* how my court would fall. I wouldn't let it.

"Well," Silas said after a moment, his one brow raised in challenge, "They've stopped."

I swallowed past the lump in my throat. "Stand," I shouted, my voice cracking.

My nails dug into my palms and an anxious sweat slicked the back of my neck, staining my ears red.

Breathe, Liana...

I steeled myself, allowing the anger and the frustration that had been begging to be set loose within me rile into something like courage. "I know you're afraid," I called out into the growing light of day and saw some of them come back to life at my words.

"I know you think we can't win."

The whispers began, and Silas opened his mouth to bark a command for them to come back to order, but I silenced him with a steady hand.

"You think you're walking to your deaths! That the Mad King will cut you down and take your lands—take *my* crown."

I had their attention now. Their faces a mirror of the disgust I carried like a layer of ichor on my flesh. My hands shook at my sides. The unadulterated fury rushing through my veins like a pack of wolves charging in for the kill.

I leaned in, attempting to meet as many of their stares as I could. "You. Are. Wrong."

Now or never...

In my peripherals, I noticed Alaric stop in his tracks at the sight of me addressing the Horde. See Kade and Finn emerge from the tent, bleary-eyed, trying to find where the sound of my voice emanated from. And Tiernan, stepping out of the town tavern with a group of other males, looking as though he'd drowned his own sorrow in the depths of a bottle or two.

My warriors. They needed to hear this as much as these soldiers did. And as much as I needed to say it and feel it and believe it.

We would all need to if we had any chance in this war.

"We *can* win." I stated as though it were obvious, though by the pinched noses and furrowed brows before me, it was obviously far from it.

"We are stronger," I yelled, my lungs heaving and pulse soaring, "We are smarter." Heat grew to a blazing fire in my core, coiling for the strike. Waiting for my command. "We are faster."

The shaking in my hands stopped, "And *we are more powerful!*"

I drew in a steadying breath, lifting my hands, palms to the sky. Open. Accepting. Hoping for acceptance and understanding in return.

"They told you I was Graced with the power to heal the sick and mend the wounded. A Grace stronger than any had ever seen."

I turned to my males, finding them stone-faced, their hands curling around their weapons in anticipation of having to use them.

Please don't see me as a monster... I sent out the silent plea. *See me as what I am...*

A weapon to wield against our enemy.

"That was a lie," I growled, "I *can* heal... but I can also do *this*—"

I raised my hands higher, projecting a column of flames from my palms, chased from my core by anger and hatred. I screamed my fury until the release was over and it left me breathing hard and fast.

"And *this*," I hissed through clenched teeth, forming twin blades of the strongest ice in my grip. I spun, slicing at a wooden training post stuck in the ground behind us. Reduced it to splinters.

Before the splintered wood could fall to the ground, I flicked my fingers. My Grace of air whirled through me like a vortex, spinning out through my fingertips to send the chunks and bits of wood spiraling in to the air above us. There I held then in a spinning torrent of wind.as though the ability had been there all along. It hadn't ever left me. It was innate. A reflex.

"And this."

Propelling the wind from me, I tossed the pieces through the air, sending them flying to land crashing into the woods behind the village. The moment I let go of the Grace, my head spun, and my breathing became more shallow.

Spots of blue and black danced in the corners of my eyes. But I bared my teeth, planted my feet to the ground and stood tall. They couldn't see me weak. They had to think me strong, Unbreakable. Fearsome and more powerful than any queen they'd followed before.

As my eyes struggled to focus and my healing Grace tried and failed to repair whatever damage I'd just done, I saw them. The fear of the unknown was plain on their faces.

Alaric's hand closed around my upper arm, pulling me back from them. Fear led people to do foolish things. But they were smarter.

They were denizens of Night. *My* people. I had more faith in them than that.

A *clang*! rang out from the group. The jarring sound of flesh and bone on metal. I found her face in the throng of warriors. With her closed fist and eyes gleaming with wild devotion she pounded on her breastplate. A sign of respect.

And then another joined her.

Another.

Until the cacophonous rattling of metal and impassioned roars filled the village. My head. The world. I clutched Alaric for support, my chest so *full* it was near bursting.

With wonder in his gaze and mouth parted in awe, Silas didn't take his eyes off me as he raised his sword high in the air, "Move out!"

CHAPTER TWENTY-FOUR

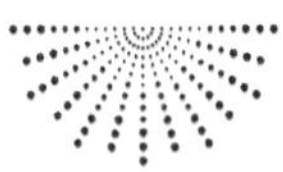

ALARIC

She'd slept most of the day after we'd sequestered her away from the prying eyes and jabbering maws of Silas and the other Fae in the village. She'd fallen onto the bed and drifted back into sleep within seconds. Her breathing shallow and skin paled.

Finn said we should send for a healer, and I wanted to agree, but I knew she wouldn't want that. And there wasn't a healer in these parts of her court—and Loris wouldn't be arriving until the following morning to set up the infirmary.

She shouldn't have used so much power for something as rudimentary as a display for the Horde.

When Liana finally awoke it was night, and the camp was bustling with life again. The next group of soldiers had arrived, and the smell of meat roasting on an open fire had my stomach in knots with hunger. All of us had been too afraid to leave her side—afraid she'd slip into the kind of sleep you didn't wake up from…

She sat up with a hand to her head, averting her gaze from us—a blush crawling up her neck to bloom in her cheeks. Arrow cawed loudly from his new post atop the coatrack in the cabin's corner.

"Yes, I see you. Hello, Arrow," she whispered in a raspy voice, and the falcon came to land softly on the fur next to her. She patted his back, ruffled the tiny feathers on his breast.

I cleared my throat, turning to pour a glass of water.

A tickle in my mind alerted me to her gentle probe of my emotional state. I smirked. But her Grace seemed to recoil all at once and I felt the strain. Like a rubber band pulled too tightly—stretched too thin.

"Quite a show you put on," I said, kneeling next to her.

Arrow snapped at me, screeching before he took flight, landing back on his post.

She peeked up at me through her lashes, and then lifted her head fully, seeming to calm at what she saw. "Are you—" she started, swallowing, "Do you think it was a mistake?"

I shook my head, "No, I don't think it was a mistake. Word is already spreading, and the Horde is rallying for battle. They have a renewed sense of hope and a thirst for the blood of their enemies."

"But?"

"But you shouldn't have exhausted yourself like that. Using all your Graces at once. You could die of you push yourself beyond your limits, Liana. Please don't scare us like that again."

She scowled, crossing her arms over her chest, "I'll need to push myself harder than that if we're going to win," she said with a note of defiance, "When I'm on the front line, I'll have—"

My stomach leapt into my throat, "The front lines?"

"Liana, are you mad?" Tiernan said, his green eyes widening.

"You will not be going anywhere *near* the front lines."

Her jaw tightened, and she glared at me. At all of us. Moving to stand on wobbly feet with her hands on her hips. "If you think for *one second* that I will stay here twiddling my thumbs while the denizens of *my* court fight for our freedom, *you lot* are the mad ones!"

"Liana," Finn started, holding his hands out toward her in a calming gesture, but the wild-eyed Liana before us was beyond being calmed. I could sense her building rage and frustration crashing into me like an assault on my mind.

"Listen," Finn said, "I know it's hard to accept, but you have to understand—if you were to…" he cringed, his adams apple bobbing as he swallowed, "If you were to *fall* in the battle. He'll win."

I could see the gears turning in her mind, but her fury didn't dissipate, it only grew with her frustration. "But I can make a difference," she yelled, "What good am I here? Morgana bestowed her Graces on me so I could *fight*. Not so I could sit here on my ass."

She swiped the glass of water from my hand and took a long swallow, wiping the droplets off her face with the back of her hand, "Well?" she said, "Is that what you all would have me do?"

I shook my head, "No, of course not."

She looked at me with something like disappointment and it pooled in my stomach like poison, reaching up to wrap a shadowy hand around my heart.

"We've talked about it," Tiernan said, casting a cursory glance at me, Finn, and Kade. "Healer Loris will arrive in the morning to set up an infirmary. Another healer has heard our call for aid, too and will arrive shortly after. But two healers to tend to possibly hundreds of wounded…"

Her face pinched, her eyes turning from orange to something more like red, "So that's it then," she said, exasperated, throwing her hands up in defeat, "You'd have me stay here, healing the wounded instead of—"

"Instead of killing Fae?" Kade barked, finally speaking up. "Yes. We *would* have you here using your healing Grace to save the lives of your people instead of taking the lives of your enemies."

She staggered back as though the Draconian's words were a physical blow.

Raking a clawed hand over my skull, I cut my gaze back to Liana, imploring her to listen. "It's not that we think you can't handle it—you've killed before…" she winced at the memory of Thana, her emotions turning rancid with guilt and nausea. "But you are the strongest healer in all the Night Court. Think of how many lives you could save."

The muscles in her jaw tightened and twitched. She dropped her gaze, falling back onto the makeshift bed with a heavy sigh.

"The battle will not be won in one day," Finn offered.

"No, it won't," affirmed Kade.

I pulled her hand into mine, and she let me, but didn't squeeze back, sending a sliver of ice shooting into my heart. "There may come a time when you'll have to fight, Liana," I told her, "But the most bloodshed will happen on the first day of battle. Just for that one day—*please* agree to stay here. If anything happened to you out there, you'd be handing your kingdom over to *him.*"

She nodded solemnly, rising to pull on her boots and grab her jacket. One part of my mind prayed she would listen to reason. But the other part wondered if we were making a mistake by convincing her to stay. Were we being selfish?

No… every reason we had was sound and true, but that didn't mean it was the *right* path.

Liana finished buttoning her long jacket and turned just before she walked out of the tent, "I'm going to get some air," she announced to no one in particular, her head bent, and then strode from the tent into the growing dark of night outside.

"I'll go with her," Finn said after a moment.

"I'll go, too," said his twin.

I nodded to them, "Make sure she's alright."

Kade came to rest a hand on my shoulder, "It was the right choice," he said, giving me a pointed look.

"Was it?"

His jaw tightened. His only reply was a squeeze to my shoulder before he followed his brother from the tent.

CHAPTER TWENTY-FIVE

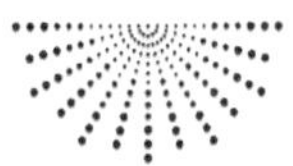

KADE

She stood there looking lost, her hands tucked under her arms to keep them warm, her breath clouding in the chill night air. She spun to the sound of our steps as we approached her. Said nothing, just stared.

"Come with us," I said to her, holding out my arm.

After a moment she threaded her arm through mine, shivering against the warmth of my skin. The three of us set off into the heart of the village. Even though it was late, there were soldiers milling about, huddling over fires, or drowning their worries in steins of ale. The village was nothing like I remembered it.

It was on these once barren streets that Finn and I grew into adolescence. I scowled at the memories catapulting to the forefront of my mind. The Fae here never really accepted us, and all but shunned us after the Alchemists slaughtered our parents at Mt. Ignis. No one knew what to say, or how to react.

We stayed for a year after they passed, until the change made us immortal, and we drafted ourselves into the Horde army—looking for any sort of escape from the dead-end place we'd once called home. It took only three years for us to become some of the best warriors the Horde had. And only a year after that Queen Enya took notice. Inviting us to drink of the waters of the Sidhe.

The nobles were outraged that we—two orphaned Draconian war dogs were given the right that was reserved only for nobles. But we'd earned it. And if we hadn't been deserving, those who'd died long before wouldn't have Graced us.

"Where are we going?" Liana asked, her voice monotone.

I tsked her, wrapping her icy hand in my warm one.

"You'll see," Finn answered, "It isn't much further.

Once we'd passed the main part of the town and turned west into the sparsely wooded forest, the cabin came into view. Squatting amid the trees. The roof caving in. The front porch overgrown with weeds and vines.

As though sensing exactly what the place was, Liana jerked her chin up to meet my steady gaze. "Is this?" she asked, looking to the cabin and back to me. To Finn.

"It was our home. Before."

It stood empty all the many years since we left it. We'd never even attempted to sell it. And if we had, no one would have made an offer. If the location didn't deter them, the whispers surrounding it would've.

The Fae who lived there before us fell in the battle of Mt. Noctis. And then our parents fell in the slaughter at Ignis. The townsfolk in these parts were prone to a superstitious nature. But Finn and I knew better. It was just a house. And the last place where a small piece of our parents was preserved.

The wood creaked and groaned as we ascended the three steps up to the front door. Finn shouldered it open, and we stepped into the dark.

I ignited my Grace, letting short flames twirl around my upheld hand, lighting the single room the cabin held.

Liana pulled her arm out from mine and took a good look around. Her gaze roving over the three beds, one large and two smaller. The hearth still covered in ash and black stains. And the small table where we shared our meals, four stools still set around it.

It had been years, and yet every time I came here, it was like coming home. I could still feel the warmth of the hearth on my younger self's face as I stared into the glowing coals, waiting for mom's veal stew to be ready so I could devour bowl after bowl until my stomach was near bursting with fullness and dad had to carry me to bed because I'd fallen asleep at the table again.

I blinked away the memory, letting the fire and steam within me burn out the ache in my gut. Finn and I would never voice it out loud, but we'd both waited for this moment since the day the news came about our parents. It was why we'd conscripted. To take revenge on the race of man that took them from us.

And now was our chance. So then why was it so bittersweet? Was it because it wasn't our lives they were after? They worked in service of the Mad King and their goal was to take the throne of night, probably to *live* in our territory. But in order to do that—they would have to kill Liana.

It wasn't about revenge anymore, not really.

It was about protecting what mattered most.

Her eyes brimmed, and she turned back to Finn and I. "It reminds me of home," she said in a whisper. And I knew she didn't mean the palace. She meant her home on the isle among the seven sisters. In the twenty-two years she spent there, they'd become her family. I wondered if she missed them as fiercely as we missed ours.

"You'll go back there, someday," I told her.

It was a promise I intended to keep.

"Stay here with me tonight?" she asked, and my lips split into a smile.

Finn smiled, too. "I'll go find some food and drink," he offered, and turned to head back the way we'd come.

"I'll start the fire," I said, kneeling near the small hearth where several dry logs sat in a basket, waiting to bring light and warmth to the desolate place.

CHAPTER TWENTY-SIX

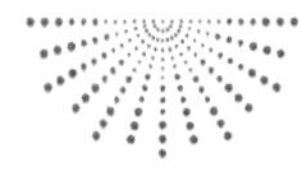

LIANA

I'd drifted off, the black furs covering the stiff bed swallowing me into their soft warmth. Kade and Finn had pressed the other beds tight on either side of mine, laying next to me, though I didn't think they slept.

The alarm sounded just after dawn, and the blaring echo of the horn resounded in my bones. I shot out of bed, eyes wide and searching.

No. Not yet...

Kade was up in an instant, tugging his boots on. Finn hurried to buckle his sword and scabbard to his waist. I shook my head. It couldn't be happening already. It should've taken another few days at the very least for the Mad King's army to reach the borders of my court. We weren't ready.

I wasn't ready.

Panicked, I inched out of the bed, my chest heaving, and mind swirling, "What's happening? Are they here? Have they come?"

Kade snarled, tossing me my boots. "No," he said, "The horn was only blown once. It means they're getting close, and every able bodied Fae is to move to the front."

"Come on," Finn said, holding out a hand for me once I'd tied the laces. I took his icy cold hand in my own and we flew from the warmth of the cabin, taking off from the ground. Finn swung me into his arms and we were at our tent in less than a minute.

I jumped from his embrace and raced into the tent. Alaric jumped from his seat, sword drawn. When he saw it was just me, he scabbarded it again and threw a hand through his hair, "There you are," he said with a sigh of relief. "Healer Loris is here. I told her you agreed to help. She's waiting for you at the mill. They're setting up the infirmary there."

I ground my teeth but nodded. "Have you seen Silas?"

He nodded grimly, "They've been spotted just past the valley. They'll be within reach of our arrows by sundown."

A tremor stumbled up my back—radiated down my arms and settled in the violent shaking of my hands. My heart fluttered in my chest and my stomach turned sour. The skewers of boar we'd eaten the night before threatening to come back up.

"Any word from Edris?"

"No," Tiernan answered, slipping into the tent with Kade and Finn behind me. "Nothing."

So, this was it, then. I hadn't truly dared to hope, but now it was clear. The Day Court wouldn't help us.

I blew out a breath. There was no use wallowing in it. We had work to do. Steeling myself, I clenched my hands into fists, "Then we have about eight hours to get that infirmary ready to take in our wounded. Let's get moving."

WE WERE silent while we worked, the constant sound of marching boots filling our ears. Loris thanked me for offering my aid.

Shortly after we arrived at the mill, which had a long hall attached to it, the other healer arrived. But it wasn't a woman like Alaric thought. The male had a fair complexion, light hazel eyes, and a placid disposition.

He radiated calm. And in the face of what we'd soon see, that was no small accomplishment. His name was Eros, and he worked diligently and quietly, keeping mostly to himself.

There was just one more thing that needed to be settled before I could take a free breath.

They hadn't said a word, but I could see it in their eyes and feel it exuding from them in ribbons of emotion. My guardians were anxious. It was obvious to anyone with two eyes and half a brain.

Kade and Finn especially. They wanted to join the fight. I saw them looking out the small windows, watching the ebb and flow of the marching soldiers.

They wouldn't go without my permission. But could I deny them the chance at retribution? Could I deny my court their two *best* warriors in one of the largest battles ever seen on Meloran?

I grew faint at the idea of letting them go. I pictured it. Saying goodbye, not knowing when or *if* they would return. My stomach twisted painfully. There was one other reason they would give for their need to join the fight. Me.

Not only to protect me and my crown, but so I could *see* through their eyes the outcome of the battle. And give orders from the relative safety of the village.

Kade looked out the window again, longing in his eyes, his chest heaving. His teeth grinding.

I tossed the pile of cloth I was tearing into bandages onto the table, "That's it!" I howled, my skin bristling, "Out. All of you."

Eros raised a brow at me, "Not you," I said a little more roughly than I intended, "Them," I clarified, pointing a finger at the four wide-eyed males helping with menial tasks like sweeping and boiling water and cleaning surgical knives.

"But—" Alaric began.

I jerked my chin toward the door, "Out," I said again, more firmly, and he and the rest of them dropped what they were doing with exaggerated sighs and rolls of their eyes to stomp out into the cold.

"What is it?" Alaric asked the moment we were outside.

"Ask," I said, leveling my gaze him, letting it flit to the others. "I know what you all want—so ask me."

I crossed my arms. Tried to quell the fire raging to life within my core.

Kade stepped forward, swallowing, "We should be at the front."

"And I shouldn't?" I snapped.

"Liana, you *can't*."

I shook my head, "Why? Because it isn't safe? Because I could *die*? Well so could any of you!"

"It's not the same and you know it," Finn said, a dangerous tone to his voice I'd never heard from him before. It wasn't longing I saw in him. It was pain. And I knew the only way he'd be rid of it.

Maybe he's right... but I didn't have to like it.

"Go, then!" I yelled, "Go, if you want to go. I won't stop you."

"Liana," Alaric said tentatively, stepping in. Reaching out.

I recoiled from his touch, "If *anything* happens to any of you..."

"Tiernan will stay here with you," Alaric said, the commanding tone of captain seeping back into his voice. My blond warrior stiffened, his lips pursing and fists clenching, but he said nothing.

That was it, then? They would go. There were *actually* going to leave me.

"We'll come back," Finn said, nodding to himself as though it was him who needed the convincing, "I promise."

"Don't make me promises you can't keep."

I couldn't say goodbye to them. I *wouldn't*. I took in the sight of them, their polished steel and leather armor covering the taught and coiled muscle below. Alaric's steel-blue eyes, the color of a winter sky. Kade and Finn's honey brown eyes that glowed gold when they took flight, or when they used their Graces. The shapes of their faces.

They were the strongest warriors in the Horde. And Alaric was a leader of his own regiment when he was in the Horde army, too. They'd come back, wouldn't they?

My lungs ached, and my heart rebelled against the thought of them leaving, squeezing painfully in my chest—making my eyes sting with tears.

"Go before I change my mind," I spoke through gritting teeth, unable to meet any of their gazes. And when none of them moved right away, I clenched my fists and shouted, "Go!"

…and then they were gone, and I collapsed into the dirt, clutching at my chest. The tearing there almost too much to bear. Tiernan's arms came around me, stoking my back. My hair. Whispering sweet words of reassurance I couldn't hear.

They would come back.

They had to.

CHAPTER TWENTY-SEVEN

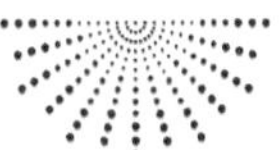

LIANA

Killing does something to your soul. Tears it. The damage is irreparable. I knew because I'd killed Thana. And I would carry that scar—that *black mark* on my soul forever. Which is how I knew if—no—*when* they returned, even if they didn't bear physical scars, they would bear mental ones. They wouldn't be the same warriors who left the small village.

War changed the hearts of men—that's what the seven sisters taught me. Would this war change me, too? *If* I survived long enough to see it through?

I slammed the bucket of water down onto the table, letting it slosh over the sides. Dipping the brush in, I scrubbed at the rough wood-grain of the table. But the water kept freezing, and then boiling, and then freezing again. I threw the scrub brush back into the bucket and rested my palms on the table, trying to catch my breath. The wood froze solid under my fingertips.

They'd left almost an hour ago. If they'd flown, and I was certain they would've, they'd be there already… at the front lines. Had the battle already begun?

Loris laid a hand on my back, recoiling at the frostbitten skin. "Oh dear," she said, "I hardly believed it when I heard…"

She came around to the other side of the table to look me in the eyes, "We stand a half-decent chance in this war, you know," she said.

I looked up, the annoyance gone, and some tension easing from my shoulders, my heart beat slowing. I cocked my head at her.

With a small awkward looking smile—*gods,* had I ever seen her smile, before? Did I look so awful that even grumpy old Loris felt she had to do something to raise my spirits? I groaned. Shook my head.

"It's true," she said, her brows narrowing, "The Alchemist race are skilled in the arcane arts. Magic. But they aren't much stronger than the men of the mortal realms. They are smart and cunning, but on the ground, if you put one Fae warrior against one Alchemist, the Fae will win. We are stronger than them. Faster, too."

I hung my head. They were my own words. Though she hadn't been here to hear them. I had convinced a legion of Horde soldiers we could win this war using a variation of those same words. They were true after all. We *were* stronger and faster. But every Fae on the battlefield would need to kill at least *two* for us to stand a chance.

And the marching continued outside the infirmary... the entire Horde hadn't even made it to the front lines yet.

And they had some Fae on their side. And Draconians. And the Mad King himself... would he be on the battlefield?

I should have gone.

I should have insisted.

Alaric. Kade. Finn.

I was back in the ruined palace at Mt. Noctis. Watching as Ricon toyed with them as though they were puppets in his morbid theater. I remembered the punch of Kade's blade as it found purchase in my flesh. The look in his eyes.

"I should have gone," I whispered to myself.

Loris placed her hand atop mine, "It was the *smarter* course to stay behind, majesty. And there's no sense regretting your decision. It'll be too late by now."

Tiernan came back into the room from where he was helping move beds and tables into place in the main hall.

"Check on them," he said, "I can see it's driving you to madness—just check on them already."

"But—"

But what if I distract them, I was going to say, but he interrupted, "The battle won't have begun yet," he said, "Trust me—the earth… I would sense if it had begun."

His Grace. I wondered what it would be like to feel the pulse of the land beneath your feet…

Biting my lips and hauling in a steadying breath, I closed my eyes. Searched for the three tethers. Found them stretched taught, tugging at my soul.

Alaric, I called down the bond, *where are you? Have you made it to the front?*

There came no answer.

"He isn't answering me!"

Tiernan came to stand next to me, covering my hand with his on the table. "Try again,"

Healer Loris gasped, realizing what I'd done. How I'd bonded myself to them.

I didn't care if she knew. I didn't care if anyone knew anymore. As long as they came back.

I'd tell the whole damned world. I'd shout it from the skies.

Alaric, I spoke again through the bond.

His voice ricocheted back to me, *they're here.*

Show me.

Concentrating, I focused on wrapping all of myself around that one tether, and the moment Alaric opened the connection—what he saw flashed against my closed eyelids.

A line of men and Fae stretching as far as I—as *he* could see in either direction between the split in the short mountain range separating the Wastes from my court. Ten thousand men and Fae. A small legion of Draconians hovering restlessly above them.

The sheer size of Ricon's borrowed army stole all the breath from my lungs.

Some were armored with sword and shield. Others looked to be… chanting? They held bottled substances in their hands. Drew glowing sigils in the air with their fingers. They were getting ready. Setting wards and drawing strengthening magical sigils like Finn said they would.

The force was no more than five hundred yards from where Alaric stood next to Silas, in our own front line of Fae soldiers.

What would happen now? What were they all waiting for?

The anticipation curdled my bloods in my veins.

What happens now?

They aren't within reach of our archers… We wait for them to initiate the charge, they have to file through the pass, it's to our advantage to wait on this side. They are waiting for us to do the same.

It began to snow. The fat flakes of it drifting down from the sky like ashes.

A hair-raising battle cry rang out from the opposing side, and my breath caught.

They charged. Screaming and chanting and sprinting across the frozen ground, their shields out and swords raised.

Silas hollered, "Hold!"

"Hold!"

Alaric drew his sword.

I love you.

And I was thrown from his minds-eye, landing back into my own mind with the force of a catapult. I fell back onto my behind hard, landing with an *oomph* on the hard wooden floor of the mill. I struggled to refocus my eyes, grasping at the tether, but the connection had faded. It was gone.

"It has begun," Tiernan said with shadows over his eyes.

CHAPTER TWENTY-EIGHT

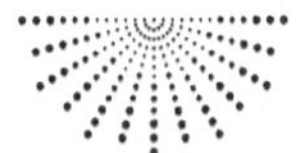

TIERNAN

The earth bled.

The moment they charged, I felt the vibrations. And at the first spilling of blood, Meloran recoiled and wept.

Liana alternated between ice and fire. Unable to control herself. She wouldn't let me near her for fear she'd hurt me. She struggled to catch her breath, looking for all the world like she was suffocating. I'd seen that level of panic before. I'd experienced it myself the day I found out my parents would never return home.

The feeling like the world is crushing you. That there isn't enough air in the room—in the entire universe to fill the gaping chasm inside you.

"Liana," I said, trying again to get nearer to her.

"I shouldn't have let them go!"

"You *need* to calm yourself."

"Get her out of here before she burns the whole infirmary to the ground," Healer Loris said, and I gave her a cutting glare so deep she ran to the other section of the mill.

As though Liana heard her, she ran out into the street, and I followed on her heels, chasing her out into the cold. I shivered, an icy flake of snow landing on the tip of my nose. I brushed it off. I'd heard of snow, but living so far to the south like I had my whole life, I never thought I'd see it.

The Horde army had all passed through the village—the last of them would be arriving at the gap now. The absence of them was like a held-breath. Leaving the streets silent. Their tent-flaps billowing in the gentle breeze.

I grabbed Liana by the arm, wincing when the icy chill of her flesh stung my palm and stiffened my fingers. "Liana, stop!"

She tried to jerk her arm free, but I wasn't about to let go—no matter how much it hurt. I bared my teeth as the frost crept up my wrist, winding around my arm.

Liana gasped at the sight of what she was doing and the cold left her all at once. Retracting from my arm as she forced a healing warmth to radiate over her body. She fell to her knees and cried softly. She was still so very young.

She hadn't had to see war, or famine, or any of the awful things of the world until only recently. I bet sometimes she wished she'd stayed on that island in the middle of the sea.

"I'm sorry," she whispered.

"You have nothing to be sorry for."

"I can't reach him… he isn't answering my calls. None of them are," she wiped at her nose with her sleeve, "Does that mean—"

"No," I said fiercely, unwilling to believe it myself. It wasn't only Liana who had become like family to me, and I refused to believe they had fallen… "You would have felt it," I rationalized, "Alaric said the severing of the bond was one of the most painful, awful things he'd ever endured, and that bond only went one way."

She leaned into me, and I wrapped my arms around her. We stayed like that for what could've been hours. Huddled together in the cold. The snow falling gently around us.

After a time, she jerked, whipping her head up, "I remember Finn saying something about a female who would see through the eyes of her bonded mate without him opening the connection. Do you remember?" she said animatedly, her eyes wide, "The story about the female who bonded herself to a male without his knowledge and was plagued by images of him with another lover in her dreams!"

"That's it!" she exclaimed before I could answer, "They won't answer me if they're in the heat of battle, but if I try hard enough, I should be able to see through their eyes, right?"

I shrugged, "It's worth a try. Here," I said, holding out my hand, "I'll open the connection between you and I—then maybe I can see what you're seeing."

She shoved her hand into mine and immediately shut her eyes, her brows pulling together in fierce concentration. *Gods*, even when she was frantic and had been crying for hours, she was still the most beautiful creature I'd ever seen.

The connection rendered me blind for an instant before the both of us jumped as she latched on to… on to *Finn.* The Draconian dove through the sky, shooting bolts of ice from his hands like lances— they tore through unsuspecting Alchemist soldiers on the ground, staking them to the cold earth.

I could almost taste the smoke—the metallic tang of blood on my tongue. Corpses littered the battlefield, the carnage jaw-dropping in its magnitude. Bodies, thousands of them—*thousands* of lives lost on both sides. As Finn spiraled up through the air, evading from an attack of lightning from another Draconian, I caught an aerial view of the battle below.

We weren't winning.

Liana's hand squeezed mine tightly, and I knew she saw it, too. Our dwindling numbers. And their forces pushing through the gap and onto Liana's territory.

Sparks of foreign power lit the ground below where the Alchemists attacked our Fae. A volley of arrows from our side of the battle blotted out the moon, finding their targets in the advancing troops of the Mad King's force.

But Finn didn't see it coming, he dove, but he was a second too late. A stray arrow found purchase in his shoulder—blowing through flesh, muscle, sinew, and bone.

Liana shouted, and the connection broke. She scrambled to get it back, and we were thrown into the battle again, this time through the eyes of Alaric as he cut down foe after foe with his dual wielded swords. Wheezing, his breath puffing around him in great white clouds.

He looked up, and we saw Kade as another Draconian knocked him from the sky, sending him plummeting down to meet the ground.

"Call them back," I shouted to Liana, "Do it now! It's a slaughter—we can't win. You have to—"

But she was already doing it, screaming down the bond to Alaric, I could hear her too.

Fall back! she said. *Do it now! Give the order!*

The momentary distraction was all the Alchemist needed to strike Alaric across the back with his blade. Knocking the wind from his lungs and us from his mind.

But the connection was still there and after a moment of grating silence, his voice came weakly down the bond, *I've given the order.*

We exhaled together, Liana slumping against me—utterly spent.

The crunch of boots and the flapping of wings preceded the shouts calling for a healer. The wounded had begun to arrive.

I watched as Liana's focus narrowed and her jaw tightened. After a single shaking inhale, she flew into action, springing to her feet. "Bring the wounded inside," she told them, and ran back into the mill.

CHAPTER TWENTY-NINE

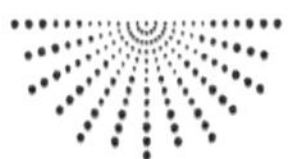

LIANA

The wounded just kept coming.

One after another after another. I couldn't heal any of them fully, just enough to save them from the edge of death, or to lessen some of the pain. But even rationing my Grace as I was, I could already feel it dwindling, and the line of wounded still to be seen continued to grow. Several Horde soldiers were already dead by the time I got to them.

I'd had to stop to vomit into a basin or a bucket twice already. The smell was foul and cloying. There was so escaping it.

But still I pressed on. Tiernan followed me from soldier to soldier, doing what he could to help. Holding them still. Giving them water, or something to bite down on when my Grace of healing wouldn't work fast enough, and I had to cauterize open, oozing wounds.

I laid my hands on one of the males laying against the wall. The arrow through his chest had missed his heart by a hair but had punctured one of his lungs. Tiernan snapped off the tip and yanked it through him while I set to work mending the tears in the fragile tissue of his lung. He would continue coughing up blood until he got it all out, but I made it so no more could seep in. I let my hands fall away from him, staggering as I tried to move to the next.

Tiernan steadied me, "You have to take a rest," he said, his voice high-pitched and frantic, "You can't keep going like this."

But he was wrong. I *could* keep going. I just had to push harder. The fire was easier to command—my fury at what they had done to the Fae of my court ran wild through my veins—and I cauterized the next two patients in the blink of an eye. There was no time to administer something for the pain, so they were left screaming at my searing touch.

The sounds wrapped around my heart, settling like lead weights in my stomach.

Black spots crowded the edges of my vision and I shook my head. Catching myself before a bout of vertigo almost had me careening to the left.

Tiernan took hold of me firmly, taking my face into his hands, "Stop this!"

I shoved him off, rushing to the next, and the next, and the next. But more and more came. It was a never ending deluge of tortured pain and twisted faces.

I peeled my hands from the female warrior, leaving her with an ugly scar of raised red flesh, but at least she would live. Turning to the next patient, I caught sight of them through the haze of exhaustion. My heart stilled—then sped up again.

They stood in the doorway of the mill, each carrying a wounded soldier in with them, when it was clear to see they were the ones who needed tending.

The arrow still protruded from Finn's shoulder. Alaric winced every time he moved, and Kade's entire right arm and side were badly bruised. He could have crushed his bones. Could have internal bleeding from the fall...

I stepped out from the table, letting go of the ledge of it I had been using to steady myself. But I lost my balance, my head spinning violently. The black spots grew—diving in front of my eyes until I couldn't see. My head connected with something hard, and the last thing I heard was shouting from familiar voices before I could hear nothing at all.

CHAPTER THIRTY

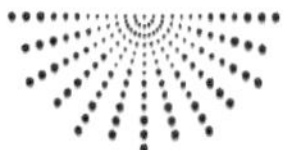

FINN

It took almost a full day for Liana to wake. And by the time she did, she found herself back in the palace, awakening in her own bed. We'd had to make some hard and fast decisions while she was unconscious. Healer Loris said with the damage she'd done to herself, it would be a miracle if she woke at all.

Liana had healed over a hundred Horde soldiers. Loris told us while she healed us she'd seen nothing like it. But Liana paid the toll —almost with her life. Alaric and the rest of us already spoke our piece to her about it. Told her if she *ever* put her life in danger like that again we'd—well, I don't know what we'd do, but she wouldn't like it.

And then the argument was over. There was no time for grudges or fighting. We'd survived the battle, and she had lived, and that's all that mattered.

"We have to think of something," she said, still bleary-eyed—her hair a mass of tangled silver, "They'll be at the front gates in a few days if not less."

We had slowed them as much as we could. Setting traps along their path to slow them and dwindle their numbers as they made their way to the palace. But still they came, and their numbers weren't dwindled enough to make any meaningful difference.

"The palace has stood for a thousand years," Alaric said, "It's hewn from the stone itself. We can wait them out."

She shook her head, "There are weak points," she said, "The main gate isn't fortified, and the Draconians can get in through any of the terraces."

"She's right," I agreed, "We wouldn't be able to wait them out for long before they found a way in."

Liana stood on shaking legs, pacing the section of floor next to her bed, "We need more soldiers." She flinched, her chin quivering.

The battle at the gap had dwindled the Horde numbers to little over a thousand, and even though she saved over one hundred of those lives… it made little difference in the face of all the lives lost.

Families had been torn apart. And they had evacuated the rest of the non-fighting Fae south with a letter bearing the queen's seal. Inside was Liana's plea to the queen of day to give them refuge. Some refused to go south—and they remained in the palace, protected by its walls for as long as they would hold.

Liana stopped, and I could see an idea forming behind her eyes. "What if we don't need more soldiers?" she asked, chewing her bottom lips, "What if we just needed *stronger* ones?"

"What do you mean?" I asked her.

"I mean—what if we had a way to make the thousand fighting Fae we have stronger?"

"I'm not following."

"The Sidhe," she breathed, her eyes widening. Gleaming. "What if we allowed everyone to drink of the waters of the Sidhe?"

"That's insane," Kade growled from where he sat on the edge of her bed.

"Is it?" I challenged him, my brain trying to solve the puzzle Liana presented it with.

Alaric stood by Kade, "It takes years to learn to control Graces given by the Sidhe."

"We don't need them to be able to fully control their Graces,"

Liana argued, "They just have to have them. When I was first Graced—my Graces came out only in times of dire need. With—with Thana, and when I had to heal Kade. Was it not the same for all of you?"

The others didn't answer, but I did, "It was," I told her, "My Grace of ice was uncontrollable, but it only manifested in situations of need in the beginning."

"Is it not worth trying?" she asked the others.

Tiernan pursed his lips, "I think so," he said. "We can't defeat them as we are now. We'd be fools not to try it."

"The Sidhe is reserved only for nobles," Alaric said, "The council will be outraged."

"Why? Why shouldn't every Fae be able to drink of its waters?" Liana hissed, her gaze cutting to Kade and I, "Let the water itself decide if a Fae is worthy of being Graced. It has the power to choose who will be and who won't be. It should never have been reserved only for nobility," she laughed, "It's a ridiculous rule."

Her reasoning was met with silence, and it was Alaric who broke it, rising from where he sat in an armchair near the door, "Alright," he said, throwing his hands up as though admitting defeat, "Let's do it."

"I'll get dressed," Liana said, rushing to untie her robe.

Alaric, Kade, and Tiernan made for the door where her servant, Jaen, stood, wringing her delicate hands in her apron, "Majesty," she whispered, not meeting anyone's gaze, "That *thing* you requested… it's ready."

"What thing?" I asked her, cocking my head.

Her spine went rigid. She looked away, shrugged. "A new pair of trousers," she said dismissively, clearing her throat, "Could you…" she started, silently asking for me to leave, and turned to Jaen, "Stay and help me dress, will you?"

CHAPTER THIRTY-ONE

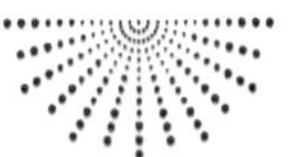

LIANA

We could see them coming. The smoke from their campfires drifting up through the trees to the north. They would be at the front gates by morning. Every able-bodied soldier in the palace, all one thousand of them had drank from the waters of the Sidhe.

Over half of them were bestowed a Grace. Flairs of power tearing through the ceremonial hall. Fire. Ice. Wind. Earth. Water. Lighting. There was no end to the scope of Graces. One Fae seemed to be Graced with the ability to commune with animals, and she had a rather lengthy conversation with Arrow about mice.

One was Graced with shadow—the rarest of all Graces. *That* had the noblemen of the council sitting up and paying attention.

I could feel they had already begun to soften to the idea of sharing the Sidhe with all Fae. The results were undeniable. If they meant it for nobility only, why then did the water chose to Grace peasants?

It was working. I couldn't help but smile watching Fae after Fae drink from the waters. The surge of power reinvigorating them, bringing light back into their war-hardened stares. There was no way to know if it would be enough. They now outnumbered us three to one, which was even worse odds than we began with.

But this time, I wouldn't be waiting in the infirmary for the wounded. I cursed myself every waking minute of the day I allowed myself to stay behind and I wouldn't do it again. This would be the final battle and it would decide the future of my court.

I would fight.

And if I died, I'd at least have the solace of knowing I died fighting for the lives of my people and the freedom of the Night Court. I tapped my pocket where the trinket from the smithy weighted down my jacket. I hoped I'd get to use it before the end.

With dawn mere hours away, we were all restless. We'd checked and double-checked everything. They had reinforced the main gate. The Horde had been fed with provisions from the royal stores. Blades had been sharpened, and arrows were still being crafted. Armor repaired. The practice ring was buzzing with activity—filled with Fae trying to hone their new Graces and learn how to wield them on command.

In the relative calm of my chambers, I felt useless.

At least Kade and Finn had Silas' call to answer and left to help him in his last ditch effort to slow Ricon's army. But I was to remain here. And Alaric and Tiernan would stay with me.

I took a slow sip of the warm spiced wine, reveling the burn as it slithered down my throat. Tiernan and Alaric sat with me in the parlor, both seemingly transfixed by the fames in the hearth. Their brows narrowed, and jaws taught. Hands clasped together, and bodies tense.

Tiernan's golden hair shone with strands of copper in the fire-light, and his green eyes looked more hazel. The fire cast shadows over his sharp-angled features.

Alaric's chest heaved with his sigh, and I noticed—I think for the first time—how the stubble on his face had grown a bit longer. Strands of deep chestnut, blackest onyx, and bits of fiery amber and gilded gold all blended together into a lovely warm deep brown. The short beard suited him. Took some sharpness away from his jaw and brought color to his usually paler features. Made his steel-blue eyes seem brighter.

Looking at my guardians, I realized there was still one last thing —a last request I would see fulfilled before dawn broke over my palace and we were at war again.

Rising from the chair where I sat between them, I turned to go back to my chambers, untying and discarding the robe covering my bare body as I went. I glanced back, finding the pair of them leaning over the arms of their chairs, wide-eyed. Perhaps a little confused.

"Well?" I said, beckoning them forward with nothing but my haughty stare. A cool breeze whipped through the parlor, hardening my nipples and lifting the hair from my shoulders. "Are you coming, or not?"

They shared a look before tripping over themselves in their haste to stand, straightening their jackets when they finally found their footing, eyes ablaze with hunger of a different sort.

I reached out my hands to them. One for each. Alaric took my left, gasping as the strength of the desirous emotions coursing through me rushed into him. The insatiable *need.* He whipped his gaze back to meet mine, his brows pulling together.

At first, I thought perhaps it was foolish—but as his expression changed to match mine, I changed my mind. It wasn't a foolish desire to want to lie with him one last time.

I caught my bottom lip between my teeth. Worked to soothe the shiver of pleasure snaking down my spine. Reached out and took Tiernan's hand in my right.

He jolted as I allowed the emotions I felt to run through my fingertips and into him. And when the wave came crashing back, it was blended with his own desire—even wilder and stronger than my own.

I gasped. Bit my lip.

"I want you," I said to Tiernan, whose gaze deepened, and his fevered breathing increased, "And you," I said to Alaric, who shuddered as I ran my hand up the inside of his wrist, over the bulge of his bicep, bringing it up to rest gently against the pulse at his neck. "I want both of you... *now*—before..."

"Don't say it," Tiernan ordered, his voice husky and commanding. He pulled me to him, crushed his lips against mine. I moaned loudly against his mouth, and he slipped his tongue between my teeth, coaxing another moan from somewhere deep in belly. My skin flushed, and my toes curled.

A forceful tug on my other hand ripped me away from Tiernan, my already swollen lips meeting Alaric's with a passion that stole the breath from my lungs.

There came a loud groan and my eyes fluttered open to see Tiernan kicking the low table out of the way, leaving the plush rug beneath our feet bare. Alaric moved to kiss the corner of my mouth, my jawline, my neck. Down to my collarbone, and the place right above my breasts.

Tiernan took hold of my wrists, binding them in his strong fingers. He lowered me to the floor and Alaric followed, settling over me when Tiernan jerked my clasped hands up high above my head and held them firmly in place. My sex wetted at the restraint and the anticipation. My back arched, and my body writhed, begging without the need for words to be touched.

Alaric's famished stare climbed my body from my neck, all the way down to my navel and then lower still, his eyes leaving a trail of gooseflesh in their wake as though the touch were physical.

I hadn't known how badly I needed this. How badly we *all* needed this. This one last escape before...

Alaric grabbed me by the ankles, his lust radiating through the soles of my feet and up through every nerve ending in my body. I cried out. He split my legs. Licked his lips, leaving them glistening in the light from the hearth.

He knelt between my legs, lowering his body to the ground. He all but disappeared beneath the mounds of my breasts. His hand lazily stroking the smooth skin of my inner thigh.

I sucked in a breath. Tiernan rearranged his hands to hold both of mine in one of his. He grasped my chin, jerking my head back roughly, but not painfully, to meet his haughty stare. "Look at *me*," he said, and his jade eyes glinted with fire.

Alaric's fingers entered me, and my eyes closed, my body shuddering at the release. Tiernan's grip on my chin tightened, and my eyes flew back open. His mouth claimed mine at the same time Alaric's mouth closed over my clit. Ravenously. Tongues swirling, flicking. Tiernan's hand slithered down my neck to rub my breasts. Palm my hardened, aching nipples. Tug and twist them. Meanwhile Alaric was working magic with his tongue and fingers.

I writhed and tugged at my arms, trying unsuccessfully to pull my hands free so I could touch them. But Tiernan wasn't having it, and I found that the tightening of his grip brought another sort of pleasure. It rippled through me, the sense of being not in control in the most beautiful way.

The heat grew in my core, but I tempered it, kept it bearable. Alaric circled my opening with his tongue, easing his fingers out and then sharply back in. Again, and again until I was left weakened and moaning. Finding my end at the same time Tiernan bit down on the sensitive skin just below my ear.

Pieces of me I'd thought were dead, numb, reignited into life.

The orgasm rocked me, and I was dizzy from the force of it. When my head stopped spinning, I realized we had moved. My hands were free, and I was lying on my side, facing the still burning flames of the hearth. Tiernan laid in front of me, his trousers had vanished, and his length pressed against my navel.

I sucked in a breath at the sight of him, a bead of moisture dripping down the head of his cock. I shivered as Alaric trailed a hand down the curve of my back, resting it in the dip above my hip bone. He grasped me, pressing his naked length against my back. I went wild with desire, my hips moving, alternatingly backing up into Alaric, and pushing against Tiernan. This. *This* is what I wanted. What I *needed*. Both of them.

My males. My guardians. My warriors.

Tiernan moved down, nudging his cock at the opening of my sex, our combined wetness arousing me to the point of mania. I could hardly breathe. Didn't know if I wanted to. I wanted him —*them* inside me. I pressed against Tiernan, the only invitation he needed.

He slammed his length into me, grasping my waist. I curled my leg over him to give him a better opening. Gasped as he filled me.

Reaching back, I found Alaric's pulsing solid length, beading with his own unsated desire and stroked the length of it. Opening my Grace to *feel* both of them, physically and mentally. Alaric moaned at my touch, and I moaned at the slow, teasing thrusts of Tiernan, who blew hot breath against my nipples with each movement.

The combined lust, love, passion, and desire of all of us rose to a blinding, deafening roar inside me. And I knew I needed the joining of us all. Discerning my need, Alaric whispered huskily at my ear, his breath hot and tingling the small hairs on my neck, "Are you sure?"

I moaned, nodding, gasping, "Yes."

I release him, and he gently probed my other opening, pressing in just slightly, before pulling back again. I sucked in a breath at the double sensation, at the slight prick of pain. But he eased himself inside slowly, little by little, until the both of them were fully inside me. I growled hungrily, my nails digging hard into the flesh of Tiernan's back at the fullness. It was almost too much.

My body convulsed, and I fed off their twin desires, their own growing need for release. And I moved, rotating my hips, moving up and down. Feeling both of them sliding in and out together in perfect harmony. The pressure of the building release expanded with me, filling every bit of me. Tripping and tumbling through my every nerve as I moved faster and faster.

Alaric's grip tightened on my hip, and Tiernan's mouth opened in ecstasy as he stared directly into my eyes. "Come for us," he commanded, and. I. Exploded...

The release coming so swiftly, rocking me so hard, I lost all the breath in my lungs in one thunderous moan. They came with me, calling out their own release. Their bodies coiling around me, tensed, and shaking.

And I was left quivering between two chests of solid steel, wrapped in the safe, warm arms of my loves. Drifting like a spark of flame carried off in a gentle breeze.

153

CHAPTER THIRTY-TWO

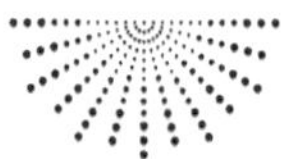

ALARIC

*E*ven with their dwindled numbers, Ricon's army was still a sight to behold. The trap Kade and Finn had helped Silas put in place—which consisted of using up all the palace's stores of pitch, and Kade's Grace of fire—had taken out another hundred. But that still left us outnumbered.

From the east facing terrace we watched them breaking through the trees in the thin forest to the north like grain through a sieve. Crawling over the land like a black disease, spreading until they formed a line, a thick barrier of men and Fae as close together as teeth in a comb. My heart thudded in my chest, and my teeth were so tightly clenched I thought one might crack.

Liana stared on in horror, saying nothing. Her breath puffing around her face in gasping clouds while she repeatedly stroked Arrow's feathers. The falcon crooned, but I wasn't sure if the petting was to reassure the falcon, or if it were more for Liana to calm herself.

The others stood quietly, too. Tiernan, with his spine erect and gaze focused. Kade and Finn much the same, their wings twitching with their innate need to be airborne. I had half a mind to tell them to take Liana and run. But she would never allow it, and they wouldn't get far, anyway.

As Ricon's force came to a grating stop a few hundred paces from the palace, awaiting command, I searched through the mass of crowded bodies. Trying and failing to find Ricon.

Damn.

Where was he? It was our best chance... perhaps our only chance. To find and kill him—cut the head off the snake, so to speak. It would force them to retreat, and then the pickings would be easy. But where in the gods' name *was* he?

I wrapped an arm around Liana's shaking shoulders and she melted into my embrace, stealing some of my warmth with her frost-covered skin. After last night, Tiernan and I had held her, laying there lazily by the warmth of the hearth on the carpet. The three of us a tangle of limbs bathed in the orange glow of flame. My cock twitched at the memory of being inside her. Of seeing her give herself over to us completely. Trusting. Us entirely hers. Her entirely ours.

It was a promise of what life could be and I wanted it more than I ever wanted anything else in my long life.

I had fought the urge to sleep as long as I could, but eventually I'd found myself woken up by Finn and Kade as they came through the terrace. I'd fumbled for my sword in the shadows, until I'd seen their faces in the glow of the embers still burning in the hearth.

They weren't one bit surprised to find us as we were. Finn tucked a blanket over Liana and Tiernan's sleeping forms and lifted their heads onto a pillow. Kade stoked the fire and added a few logs. And there we'd stayed. The five of us together, waiting for dawn.

It's all happened so fast. *Too fast.* We hadn't had enough time together. And this would not be our end. I wouldn't let it.

By the looks in the eyes of the others, they were thinking the same way. It was time for the real fight, and we wouldn't stop until it was over. One way or another.

"We wait," I whispered to Liana, feeling her getting anxious, her blood buzzing with the need to go into action. To *do* something.

"We let the archers take as many of them as they can. We hold *here*, within the walls and launch our attacks."

She nodded gravely, her skin warming until it was near burning with her fury and passion. I squeezed her shoulder before I let go.

We waited, watching with the steady, single-focused gaze of a hawk. Until the sun fell lower in the sky, and I could see the moon at the same time.

Late afternoon.

What were they waiting for?

A moment later, four figures on horseback emerged from the tree line, riding to where the army waited at our doorstep.

"It's him," Liana said, leaning far over the edge of the terrace, "It has to be."

And it seemed it was. Ricon himself, flanked by three other riders. His personal guard? But they seemed short. Young. They couldn't be guards.

"Now is our chance!" Liana exclaimed, frantic as she spun to face us. "We have to kill him. Kade, help me," she made a grab for his arm, but he recoiled.

He shook his head, and she scowled at him, hissing, "What are you doing?"

"You can't go down there right now, it would be suicide."

She steamed with unspent rage but turned back to the swarm of Ricon's army below. She gasped, "Where did he go?"

I looked where I'd only just seen him—there, on the outer edge of the last wave of his soldiers. But he wasn't there. Nor were the three other riders. Only their horses remained, left to go where they pleased. He was somewhere in the thick of it. Blended in to the thousands of faces staring ahead.

The front line broke apart and a group of soldiers marched out, two lines of ten men. A battering ram between them.

"Archers!" I heard Silas call out from the lower battlement.

And then a moment later, "Loose!" Four of the twenty men fell, but they were quickly replaced. Making their way to the front gates.

"The gates," Liana exclaimed.

"I'll keep them sealed," Tiernan said through clenched teeth. He kissed Liana swiftly on the back of her hand, his eyes flicking up with the burning promise of his return.

I nodded to him, giving him permission to do what he could. There were few as skilled as he was in their Grace of earth. The garden was only just inside the main gates, he could use its trees and plants to strengthen it.

Arrow cawed after his master, the sound shrill. Liana hushed the creature, resuming her stroking, "It'll be alright," she said to him, "He'll come back. He always comes back."

But her hands shook where they stroked the feathers and the air between was filled with her panicked worry, and the foreboding sense of dread.

The sound of unified voice drifted up to us, and I looked down to see the Alchemists as they reached the gate. The archers loosed arrow after arrow, but they struck some sort of barrier, raining to the ground around their feet. The sound… they were chanting. One Alchemist stood near them but did not hold the battering ram. He led the chant, drawing sigils in front of him as though his fingers were dipped in glowing ink and he could use the very air as a canvas.

He was protecting them.

"There!" I shouted down to Silas, pointing at the one who seemed to control the strange magic, "That one! Take him out!"

But our archers' arrows couldn't penetrate his wards either.

It would only be a matter of time before they broke through. The first blow hit the gate, and the vibrations reverberated up through my heels.

Again. The vibrations harder. The poignant, blood-chilling sound of splitting wood echoed like the crack of lightning.

"They will break through!" Liana screamed.

What remained of the Horde army waited in the inner court-yard, near a thousand bodies pressed together, waiting for the attack. Silas had instructed them to remain within the walls, which would force Ricon's army to file through the gate if they managed to break through. We had a better chance that way, but I'd seen what the Alchemists could do.

It would only delay the inevitable.

I ground my teeth, clenched my fists. My heart thudded loudly in my head. Kade moved to the edge of the terrace, "We have to stop him," he growled.

Liana grabbed him by the arm, "They'll kill you!"

"Not before I burn them all to a crisp."

I nodded to Kade, and Liana choked out a sob, shoving into my chest, "You can't let him—" she started, but an ear-slitting screech assaulted our ears. As one we turned, finding Arrow spreading his wings as the falcon dove from the railing.

Liana lunged after him, "Arrow," she called, "No, come back!"

I grabbed Liana, stopping her before she fell over the terrace.

But the falcon was almost there, it was too late. Arrow tore through the Alchemist's wards, attacking the man's face with his razor-sharp talons. Digging out his eyes. The Alchemist raised his hands to shield his face, screaming out at the assault. A glowing light pulsed out from the man's raised hand, and Arrow went rigid, tumbling from the air to connect with the ground in a plume of dirt and dust.

A lancing pain seared into my chest as the skin on skin contact between Liana and I heaved her grief and anger and anguish into me.

CHAPTER THIRTY-THREE

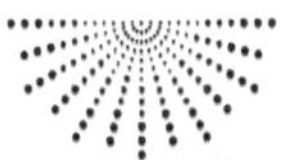

LIANA

I couldn't see him. Arrow had fallen, disappeared into a cloud of dirt at the Alchemists feet. My chest ached. Tiernan wasn't even here. He was down there, at the gates. He didn't know his companion of the last twenty years had fallen.

This time, Arrow wouldn't be nursed back to health. A hot tear dropped down my face, and the grief rapidly turned to fury in my blood.

The archers used the window of opportunity to shoot down the men still battering the gate, but more came, and the blinded Alchemist began the chant once more, his eyes ringed in dripping crimson.

Stupid. *Stupid bird! Why?*

Why did the loss of the creature open a jagged fissure in my heart?

The battle hadn't even truly begun, and I'd already had enough. I'd kill them. I'd wipe them all from the face of *my* land. The weight of the black amulet in my pocket reassured me. I searched through the crowd for his face again, for a glimpse of his shining silver hair.

Once I found him, I'd be the one to end him. It was a promise I'd made myself, and one I fully intended to keep. I wasn't sure how I'd do it yet, but when the time came, I'd figure it out.

Each blow to the gate reverberated through the palace. The stone itself shuddering against the assault of the metal tipped wooden beam. Another crack split the air, and if I leaned over, I could see they were almost through. My stomach dropped.

It wasn't supposed to happen like this. So quickly. The full force of Ricon's army began a slow march toward the gate, their shields raised from the onslaught of arrows. Silas called volley after volley, finally giving the order to fire at will in a fierce roar.

"Tiernan," I said, "He has to get out of there. They'll be through the gate any minute!"

Alaric shook his head, his expression grim, "And Tiernan is a valuable soldier who will be needed on the front lines. He knew this would be the outcome when he went down there to brace the gate."

No.

I scrambled to find the tether between us, yanked on it hard, *Tiernan,* I said down the bond, *Tiernan you have to come back. They're about to break through.*

A beat of silence.

Then I felt his answering tug in my chest.

I can't come back... It's time to fight.

Get back here! That's an order, Tiernan!

My chest swelled, and my throat burned.

He didn't answer.

My breathing came in ragged gasps, and my skin *burned.* Flames licked up and down my arms, and I was close to the breaking point.

Maybe they were right. I wasn't ready for war. To sacrifice what needed sacrificing to save my lands and the denizens of my court. Because if it meant losing *them,* how could I ever come to terms with that?

Tiernan was right.

It is *time to fight.*

If Tiernan fought, I'd fight alongside him. We'd fight together. All of us.

"Take me to the gates," I said, my voice strong and steady. Commanding. I wouldn't be kept up on this terrace like some wall-flower, forced to watch my court fall from the safety of the palace walls. *No.* It was time for Liana, *Queen* of the Night Court to show her worth.

Alaric's adams apple bobbled in his throat. His light eyes darkened.

"Take me to—"

The sound of the horn blaring out over the palace preceded the final *crack* that cleaved the gate in two. But it wasn't the swarm of Alchemists flooding into my inner courtyard, or the clang of steel on steel, or the cries of Fae and man as they were met with killing blows that drew my attention.

To the south, at the crest of the hill, a woman with hair as black as coal sat atop a brilliant white mare. She blew through the curved horn again, and Ricon's army turned toward the sound. The Draconians taking wing to get a better look. Suriel raised her sword high above her head. And the cries of a thousand voices became one unified roar as the Day Court army followed their queen to battle.

Sitting astride his own steed, Edris rode up alongside her. Armored and looking more like a king than I ever thought him. He'd done it. My *father* had done it!

The sight shocked tears from my eyes. Made my blood sing.

Alaric, Kade, and Finn stared agape.

And as one, Ricon's army trembled. Reforming a second line to face their new threat.

Suriel caught sight of me on the terrace, and I jumped to stand atop the balcony. Raising my clenched fist in the air before bringing it down to pound hard against my chest. Knocking the tears from my face and the wind from my lungs.

She called out the charge. Spurring her mare onwards faster and harder. Edris joined her, leading the charge with the Queen of Day. His battle cry rang out over the land like the mighty roar of a dragon. The Day Court army swept in behind them, clad in white and gold, they broke over the reformed front line of the Alchemists in black, like light over shadow.

The Horde had shoved through the thinned force at the gates, driving them back. A head of golden hair was my singular focus. And I watched as Tiernan danced through the chaos like a leaf caught on the wind. His sword cutting down foe after foe after foe without rest. Without stopping. His jade eyes wild, and his movements precise. Anticipating the moves of those around him long before their blades could fall.

It's time to fight.

The Day Court hadn't managed to muster their full force—that was clear form their numbers. Perhaps one and a half thousand Fae had come to our aid. This was the deciding moment. We had to hit hard and fast with everything we had or risk losing the matriarchs of two courts on this day, plunging all Meloran into darkness.

Alaric kissed me on the forehead, crushing his lips to my flesh before he pressed me into the waiting arms of Kade. "You're right," he said, "It's time to fight."

He stepped close to Finn, and the Draconian took him by the arm. He was at war with himself. Knowing he couldn't stop me from fighting but wanting so desperately for it to not be necessary. But he knew as well as I did; there was a reason Morgana blessed me with my Graces, and this was that purpose.

"I'll see you when it's over," Alaric said, his voice gruff as though he'd swallowed stones.

"When it's over," I replied.

Finn tipped his head to me, "Be careful," was all he said, conveying so much more than the mere two words in his gaze before he jumped from the terrace with Alaric in his clutches.

I spun to Kade, breathing hard. My muscles twitching in anticipation. The place in my core where my Graces emanated from roiling and bubbling and freezing and burning. Clawing at the cage of my bones and flesh, growling. Begging to be set loose.

Kade's eyes glowed yellow, fierce and piercing as he drew me in close. The flames on our skin intertwining, growing stronger as they fed from each other. "Are you ready," he asked through the crackle and pop of sparks, and the dull whooshing of fire as it licked up to my shoulders and spread over my hair.

My throat went dry. Was I? Against their better wishes I'd worn no armor save for a breastplate and gauntlets and held no weapons save for a dagger in my right boot. I wouldn't need a sword or leathers. I didn't plan for anyone to get that close to me.

"I'm ready."

CHAPTER THIRTY-FOUR

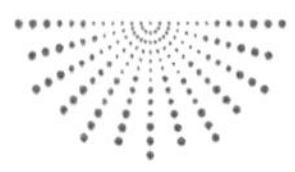

LIANA

The moment my feet touched the earth, I sprang from Kade's arms and a blade swung for my head. I dodged the attack, turned to reduce the male who wielded the weapon to ashes. "Go," I shouted back to Kade, as the other Draconians took flight. We needed him in the air, not on the ground.

"I'll be fine, go!"

I didn't turn to see if he'd listened. I didn't want for him to look at me the way the others did before I lost sight of them—like it was the last time they would. As though they were saying goodbye. I couldn't stand another look like that. I sprinted away from him, readying my Graces for a glorious release.

Men tried to stop me, swinging at me, chanting, casting spells, drawing sigils in the air. But none were fast enough, and none were prepared for what I threw at them. I bowled through them. Throwing out ribbons of flame and shards of ice. I heard their cries. Saw their anguished faces as they fell. But I roared through it. Kept going. Slaying men and Fae in a torrent of fire and ice.

I didn't have time to *feel* it. Not the way I thought I would. The loss of life. The small tears in my soul with each life I took. I felt nothing. Only fury for what they'd done to my court. And it drove me near madness. The building of flame near bursting even though I kept letting it loose from my skin. And the ice shot out of me in bolts the size of jousting lances, but *still* there was no true release.

Another man in my path. Another corpse of ash. A Draconian's assault from the sky. Left falling from the air in a block of ice. Shattering to the ground like broken glass.

I was close now. The last legion of Ricon's army marched to join in the carnage on the southern road. The Day Court army wouldn't fair well against the addition of another two-hundred men.

But they would never make it there. A slow, sneaking smile spread over my mouth. I raised my arm to set flame to the men, and gasped, the wind knocked from my lungs at the ferocity of the blow to my thigh. I cried out, releasing the hold I didn't realize I'd had on my Graces.

A torrent of wind blasted out from me, visible as it swept out over the land, knocking every soldier it hit to the ground. Leaving most unconscious and unmoving. Not what I had planned, but I'd take it.

The arrowhead jutted out from the pale skin on my inner thigh. Gritting my teeth, I snapped off its head. Sucked in a breath as I dragged it back through the way it came, my healing Grace working fast to stitch the skin closed. Erase any damage done to tendon and nerve.

And then I saw him.

Beyond the dead or slumbering bodies strewn around me like fallen flies. Silas charged for him, alone, his sword raised. His eyes shining with insatiable bloodlust.

For the smallest second, I had hope. I thought he would be able to do it. That I would watch Silas end the life of Ricon once and for all.

But I was wrong.

Silas stopped as though he'd hit a wall. His sword fell to the earth. I watched the captain of my armies' eyes widen and chest sharply expand before the Mad King lifted his sword and swung it over his head, ending Silas in one fatal cut.

His headless body slumped to the ground.

The fire burned hotter in my core. Stretching and growing.

Time to die.

My heart pounded. My blood sang in my ears.

And I moved. Feeling weightless as a feather drifting in the cold afternoon breeze. My body came back to itself all at once—heavy and weak. A taste like ashes coated my tongue. Had I… had I traveled by smoke?

There wasn't time to think on it, Ricon stood with his back to me and I had but a second before he'd sense my presence. I pulled the chain from my pocket, surprised to find it intact after resting so long against my molten skin. I supposed it had something to do with the clenched fist of bindstone clutched in the crude silver setting.

Lunging, I cleared the four running steps to him. He turned. I sprang from the ground, dropping the necklace around his head.

I had the satisfaction of watching his expression open in shock before I crashed to the ground. He raised his hands to remove the amulet, but I was faster. Freezing his hands into twin blocks of ice, the weight of his new manacles so great he crashed to his knees. His encased hands immovable as stone on either side of him.

A tingling of malice ran down my spine, alerting me to the attackers just before they could reach me. I blasted them with fire, then drew a ring of it in the sand around us. Coaxing the flames high.

Ricon's sea-glass eyes shone and his shoulders shook with silent laughter until he was gasping uncontrollably, his head bent and breaths heaving. The cackling laughter echoing all around us, mingling with the hiss and pop of flame.

"Enough," I said, and he raised his head, a tear falling from his left eye and a crazed smile on his lips.

"What are you waiting for?" he spat, his expression instantly changing from one of hilarity to one of a coarse, fury-laced growl, "Go ahead. Kill me. Become the murderer you believe me to be."

"You *are* a murderer."

His gaze flicked to the corpses at my feet, smoke still coiling up from their charred bodies. "And you aren't?" he asked me, tilting his head, his silver hair falling over half his face.

The dead man at my feet bore a ring on his left hand. I knew what it meant. That he was bonded—in their ways of the ritual. Somewhere his mate would wait for him, but he would never come home. Had he had children.

"Yes," Ricon hissed, "Murderer..."

All the emotions I hadn't granted entry before came crashing over me in great white-capped waves. How many had I killed? How many families had I broken?

No. No, they had hurt us. *They came to destroy* us.

Murderer...

I realized what was happening at the same time Alaric tumbled through the ring of flame. Batting out a lingering fire from his tunic.

"Liana," he said, relief oozing from every inch of him at the sight of me. I searched him for injury and found nothing more than shallow cuts and bruises.

He stepped forward, his jaw clenching when he beheld the monster kneeling before me.

"No, don't!" I yelled, "Even with the bindstone, he managed to get in my head."

"What are you waiting for?" Alaric asked, "Kill him."

And maybe it was wrong. But I wanted him to feel as I did when that black stone knocked against my breast. The hollow, heaviness that made me weak, and rendered me all but useless.

Just then, Kade, Tiernan, and Finn dropped from the sky into my ring of fire. Drawing their blades at the sight of Ricon.

"Are you alright?" Finn asked, looking to where the arrow had pierced my thigh. They must've felt it. And when I threw up the walls of flame, they thought it was a beacon—calling for aid.

I didn't really care why they came. Seeing them all, I was so relieved.

Tiernan kept the weight off his right leg, and Kade had what looked like a stab wound on his bare stomach. But the brute had already cauterized it closed, leaving the skin raised and red. Finn didn't seem injured at all, and I sent a silent prayer to whatever gods had been looking after my males in my absence.

"Fine," I answered Finn, stopping him and the others from approaching with a raised hand. "Don't come too close."

"So that's what you were hiding…" Finn mused, eyeing the onxy crystal hung around Ricon's neck. "You could've told us."

I shrugged, "You'd have told me it was foolish."

"I would've."

Ricon loosed an exaggerated moan, "Get on with it already. Death will be a welcome reprieve from watching you reign over *my* lands."

I tsked him. "Not so fast, *King* Ricon. I want to savor this moment."

His eyes glinted, peeking up at me, filled with the reflection of the flames all around us, and something like surprise or… pride? "Perhaps I was wrong about you…" he said, cocking his head, "I thought you were so like her, my Morgana," he shook his head, the silver hairs brushing over his forehead, "But I was wrong. You have *my* mind."

Murderer…

The jeweled hilt of the Blessed Blade caught the mottled sunlight, throwing red, yellow, blue, and green reflections against his armor. The stones near glowing with light.

Yes, I suppose that today, I am *a murderer,* I pushed the thought back to him and watched his brows raise as my voice entered his mind without physical contact. *A murderer of Night Court foes and Mad Kings.*

I reached for the blade but stopped as three dark-clothed males vaulted over the flames and into the ring with us. Alaric went to attack them, but I threw out a blast of air, shoving them back towards the flame.

Stop! The command permeated my mind, and I fought to keep my hold on my Grace of air. In awe at the Mad King's strength of power. But I kept them at bay while Alaric and the others stalked towards them around the outskirts of the flame, keeping a safe distance from Ricon. Their swords out, eyes glowing, going in for the kill.

"Please," Ricon said, and the tenderness with which he said it had my power faltering even more. "Please, don't hurt them."

Ricon's eyes held the weight of his request. Had he said *please?* He looked to the three males and back to me, silently pleading me—no, *begging* me to stop.

I recognized them. They were the ones who had ridden with him to join the battle. Two with deep chestnut hair and honey eyes, tall and thin. And the other with long silver hair tied back with a strip of leather, his face streaked with blood and dirt, but there was worry in his features. Panic.

And I realized it before he spoke the words in my mind.

They are my sons.

And Thana's... I added to his thought.

His jaw clenched, *yes.*

"Alaric, wait," I said, stopping my captain before he could make quick work of them.

He gave me a confused stare, stopping in his path—stopping the others too. But none withdrew their swords. It was taking all the energy I had left to keep the wind gusting out from me, holding the three males back.

They cursed and shouted, and I heard Thana in their voices. Saw her in their eyes. In the one on the right's slender hands, and the one in the middle's sharply chiseled jaw. They were mortal still. Not but children by Fae standards.

"What is it?" Finn asked.

My heart clenched, "They're Thana's sons," I breathed.

My hands curled to talons at my sides. Shaking. *Gods damned fool!* I wanted to scream in frustration. How could I kill her children? Even after what she'd done to me. Even if they shared *his* blood, too.

I squared my shoulders at Ricon, who had begun to shiver from the icy chill running up his arms from where his hands were still encased in thick crystal ice. The skin within the blocks turning black. "Tell them to drop their weapons."

For a moment, it was almost as though the madness left him, and I was staring into the face of a father who would do anything to save his sons. Not the monster of a moment before.

"Hand over your weapons," he called to them through my onslaught of wind, "Do as they say."

"Father!" The silver haired one shouted, his face twisting.

"Do as I say!" he commanded, and the three boys discarded their swords, daggers, and a bow onto the dirt.

"Take them," I shouted to Alaric, releasing the last of the wind from my body, my legs shaking with the effort of standing.

My guardians took hold of them, locking their arms tightly behind their backs.

"You won't kill them," Ricon said, more a question than a statement.

You can't... the thought scratched on the inside of my skull. *I know your mind, I can see inside it. I know what you hide. That a child grows within you. You can't take the lives of mine. I can see it. You won't.*

My skin turned to ice. My throat went dry. How had he known? I wasn't even certain I'd admitted it to myself. But I'd felt *strange* for days now, perhaps weeks even. I wasn't sure, and I had no way of knowing whose father the child was or if it were even true.

But he was right about one thing. I wouldn't kill them. Because unlike Ricon, I was not the sort of monster who killed children. The youngest one looked as though he hadn't even begun to grow hair on his face. No—they would live. But no where near me or Meloran.

"Take them away," I commanded Alaric, "No child should have to witness the death of their parent."

"No! Please," one begged.

"Leave him alone!" the youngest whined, his eyes brimming with tears.

But I couldn't bring myself to believe that Ricon was anything less than a monster as a father than he was a monster to everyone else he encountered. These poor young males simply didn't know any different. I told myself they would be better off without him

Tiernan drew seeds from a small pouch at his waist and bound their hands and feet quickly with thick vines he grew, weaving them around their wrists and ankles before handing them off to Kade and Finn to carry back to the palace.

The cries of battle still sounded in the distance, but they were less and further apart. It was almost over. And the skies were clear of Draconians save for a few baring the mark of the Night Court. They would be safe enough to fly back. "Be careful," I told Kade and Finn, "Take them to the dungeons."

Ricon nodded gravely to his sons, once, slowly. The only goodbye he would give them. And then they were gone. Shouting and screaming from the sky as my Draconians carried them off on black wings shining with flecks of bronze in the light of the setting sun.

"Thank you," Ricon said, bowing his head.

A half laugh bubbled up from some dark place within me. Alaric moved to stand beside me, placing a hand on my shoulder to lend me strength I didn't need. "Don't thank me," I hissed at him. The anger returning, bringing a haze to the edges of my vision.

How dare he thank me. How dare he take advantage of my kindness. After all he'd done. All the lives he'd taken and families he'd ruined. Villages he'd burned along the way. How many of my people would be left homeless because of him?

"You will still die on this day. And your children will never set foot on Meloran again."

I shook off Alaric's hand, stepped in and wrenched the Blessed Blade from his belt and the steel chest plate from his torso. His eyes bulged, the pupils constricting just before I drove the blade into his heart.

He choked, gasping, his breaths coming slower, shorter, as I knelt down to whisper in his ear, "Monsters like you shouldn't be allowed to have children. For their sakes, and for the sake of who their mother once *was*… I pray to the gods they don't turn out as *mad* as you."

The blade did its job, taking his life in swift seconds, feeding his Graces into me. The ground trembled beneath my feet and something like shadow seeped through my skin. My back arched, and my heart raced. Feeling more energized, more *powerful* than I ever had before. Alaric knocked me away from the blade, my hand slipping from its blood coated hilt.

I took a long shuddering my breath, my vision fading. The flames died around us. And when my vision returned, I found myself wrapped in the arms of Tiernan and Alaric, alone save for corpses in a ring of charred earth.

"It's over," Tiernan said, brushing my hair. "It's all over, my queen."

CHAPTER THIRTY-FIVE

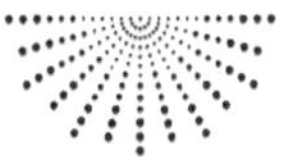

LIANA

We'd won, and yet it didn't feel like a victory.

With all the lives lost and homes ruined, how could it? One thing I knew for certain—I'd seen enough of war and woe for a lifetime.

Alaric curled his hand around mine, rubbing soothing circles into the back of it with his thumb. My other guardians waited for us in the bay. Ready with a ship meant to carry us across the Varinian Sea.

Edris sat on the other side of the oval table in the council chambers with Queen Suriel pressed against his right side. The pair looked well after several days of rest, and I wondered when the Queen of Day would go home to her own court. She didn't seem as though she wanted to leave at all.

My father pushed the parchment back across the table, pressing his lips into a hard line, "But why?" he asked.

I considered my response carefully, "Because I don't know when I'll return."

"Do you mean to return at all?" Suriel questioned, her shoulders pushed back, "After everything you've fought for, why leave?"

I couldn't tell them the whole truth of it. I hadn't even told my males yet. Thank the gods they accepted my decision without too much prodding.

"It doesn't matter," I answered, sighing. Worrying the soft fabric of my cloak. "Almost the entirety of my court has taken refuge within Day Court borders. And I thank you for that," I said pointedly to Suriel, "It will take years. Decades, if not more to rebuild what was lost here in the north."

"But, a land without a ruler—"

"My people will have a ruler—a steward of the throne of Night will remain in my stead. That is what I ask of Edris."

Alaric cleared his throat, "I'll bring the queen home safe, once she's done whatever it is she's setting out to do."

"And what is that exactly?" my father asked skeptically, one brow raised.

I shrugged, "I'm not sure yet... but the people of the Night Court have always admired and revered you. I know they will follow your lead, and I trust you to be their ruler."

Gods... I couldn't believe I'd once thought he was out to dethrone me, and now here I was—quite literally *giving* him my throne. But he wasn't like Enya, or like the other nobles at court. He was wise, and caring, and fair. He'd take good care of my court until I returned.

If *I returned,* I reminded myself. I wasn't sure yet if I ever would. My males were all that mattered to me. They were my home. And if I was being honest, I'd never quite fit into the role of *queen.* The mold was too small. Constricting.

I made a promise once, to the seven sisters on the isle where I grew up. A promise to return one day, and I longed for the quiet, tranquil solitude of that faraway place again. After that—I wasn't sure where we'd go. To the mortal lands, perhaps? I wanted to settle somewhere free and safe. Untainted by the stain of war and death.

Some place we could start anew. The five of us. Build a family together. We could decide to return someday, when the babe was grown, but that would be a decision for another time...

Looking at Suriel and Edris, I saw what my people saw—they

even *looked* like rulers. Regal. Refined. They didn't even know they'd been stuffed into molds, that their lives would open up before them with limited possibilities. And it was because they'd been conditioned to live a certain way. Take one mate. Have one Grace. Produce an heir.

And perhaps that was what they would do if I never returned. Produce an heir that could rule over both courts and form a united kingdom of Fae.

Maybe… but I wouldn't be around to watch them do it.

"I'll do it," Edris said, pulling the contract back to him. Lifting the quill. "If this is truly what you want…?"

Alaric squeezed my hand and I squeezed back, "It is."

"Then I wish you all the happiness in this life—wherever it may take you, my daughter."

And he signed.

"WE DID AS YOU ASKED," Kade hollered over the icy wind as we made our way down to the bay, "The Mad King's *offspring* left on their own ship at dawn."

"You're being generous, it was a boat. A very *small* boat," Tiernan said, crossing his arms.

Kade shrugged.

Finn came to take the satchel from my shoulder, "They didn't seem to know much about sailing. I doubt they'll make it far."

"It isn't our concern," I said to him, "For Thana, I hope they make it somewhere and start a new life. One without… well, you know."

He nodded, "I do," he said, and turned to walk the gangplank up onto the small vessel, finishing up loading the rest of our things.

We'd hidden the Blessed Blade away in the bowels of the palace —left it in the hands of Morgana far below the ground. Strange, how easy it was to find her temple chamber when I had searched and searched before. I had a feeling it was only there when I needed it. And would reveal itself for no other. I hoped I was right.

The new Graces I'd stolen from the Mad King felt strange in my core, foreign. The Grace of shadow and that of earth—I wished I could give them back to the Fae they were stolen from. But that wasn't possible. What I could do was promise their spirits one thing; I would use their Graces to do *good*. Or, perhaps, I wouldn't use them at all.

I hoped I wouldn't need to ever again.

A bout of nausea gripped me, and I swallowed back bile, curling my fist into my stomach.

"Not even on the ship yet and you're already sea sick?" Finn said, coming back down to stand with us on the dock.

I smirked, blushing.

When I didn't say anything, Alaric picked up on my emotions. The hesitation. The anxiety. The worry.

"What is it?" he asked me.

Steeling myself, I sucked in a long breath of the chill sea air. Tried to relax the tension in my shoulders.

Kade put a warm hand on my arm, and I flicked my face up to find his golden gaze staring warmly into me. He tugged gently at the tether holding us together through the Immortal Bond, "Are you alright?"

I smiled. Finding Tiernan's jade green gaze just as warm and inviting as Kade's. And Finn just as worried as Alaric.

What am I so afraid of?

"I-It's not sea-sickness," I starting, licking my dry lips, "It's—oh what did Loris call it…? Right! That's it, it's *morning sickness.*"

Finn's jaw dropped. Alaric, and Tiernan's followed suit.

Kade cocked his head at me, making a strange face that told me he was the only one who had absolutely no idea what I was on about. "What?"

Finn shoved his brother, "She's with child, you idiot."

His face burned with a bright red flush, and his eyes glowed like molten steel. He turned to me, and the flush faded. The confused look morphing into the most brilliant smile I'd ever seen him wear. He charged in and lifted me from the dock, crushing me against his wide chest before setting me back down, leaving me off balance, staggering as I tried to find my footing on the wobbly wood.

I beamed at him, and I spun to find three more smiling faces and waiting embraces.

"I love you so much," I said to all of them. "I'm sorry I didn't tell you right away—I didn't… well I wasn't sure how you would react."

Because we'd never know who fathered the child for certain. We could guess, of course. But I didn't want to. This child—*our* child would grow up with the love of four fathers. And I thought that was the most beautiful gift I could give my child.

Alaric pulled me against him, and I jolted. His emotions of excitement and pride rushing into me. And there was something else there, too. The love for his unborn son or daughter. I could already feel it within him—and if I reached out—within *all* of them.

The others crowed around us, wrapping their arms around Alaric and I until we were cocooned in warmth, shielded from the sun by my Draconian warrior's great black wings.

It was time for another sort of adventure.